THE COURTESAN OF CONSTANTINOPLE

TINA HOLLAND

ACKNOWLEDGMENTS

No project is written inside a bubble and this was no exception:

Thanks to all the Word-Weavers for their critiques – Mary Jean Adams, Maddy Barone, Laura, Patti, and Kat - you are a blessing catching every little thing.

Thanks to Krystal for catching body parts in the wrong place and asking the question "Okay, show me?" when I tried to start some SH*T!

Thanks to The Founders group - Nikki, Evey, and Rachel who were there in Las Vegas when this book was just a blink.

Thanks to A. Catherine Noon who kept asking "Is it published yet? Is it published yet? Is it published yet?" Well, Noony, here it is.

Thanks to Misty Dietz and Vania Rhealt for sharing a bit of the Indie-publishing world with me over lunch and coffee, respectively.

Thanks to Michelle and Book Boutiques for waiting with patience as I shopped this around before coming back to where I should have started.

Thanks to Misti Moyer for her editing eye.

Thanks to Valerie Tibbs for this wonderful cover.

Thanks to Scott at Other Worlds Ink for formatting the print edition as well as creating the cover wrap.

Last, but certainly not least, thank-you to My Readers. I wouldn't be able to keep doing this job I love without you. I hope you enjoy this novel.

Tina Holland
www.tinaholland.com

REVIEWS

"The Courtesan of Constantinople" dishes up a vibrant tale of steampunk fantasy and spine-tingling suspense!"

— ~IND'TALE MAGAZINE

"A fantastical blend of history (a bit twisted but still 👀) suspense, romance, and fantasy"

— ~ REVIEWER JOYFFREE ON GOODREADS

"Ms. Holland is a fantastic storyteller."

— ~A. CATHERINE NOON, AUTHOR OF CHICAGOLAND & EMERALD CITY SHIFTER SERIES AS WELL AS THE PERSIS CHRONICLES

CHAPTER ONE

1868
"The Great Britain Horizontal" Brothel
Constantinople

*L*aurel relaxed in the aftermath of Lieutenant Aaron March's passionate affections. He was an excellent lover. Of course, she was an excellent teacher. She smiled, remembering when he first came to her at the sultan's palace. He was and remained her only lover since Ben's death.

"How can you smile and look sad at the same moment?" Aaron's handsome face loomed above hers. His bright red hair stood on end from her frenzied fingers, and his brilliant green eyes bored into hers, seeking answers.

"Oh, great sir, you will find I can do many things simultaneously," she rubbed her foot along his calf.

"I'm aware, madam," he kissed the tip of her nose, before rising from the bed to put on his trousers. "Have the new girls arrived?"

"Yes. I suspect the Creole from across the pond, and the girl Emperor Meiji sent to us will both be popular." Laurel sat up. The ocean-blue, heavy satin sheet fell from her chest to pool around her hips.

"I can't imagine any woman as well trained as you, Lovey." Aaron leaned over and flicked a finger across her nipple, watching it pebble beneath his quick touch.

Laurel cringed at the endearment, not ready to have his heart. She plastered a smile on her face. "Not every madam can train with Aimee Debucq in the sultan's harem."

"Not every English girl is forced to endure such atrocities." The heat in Aaron's voice was unmistakable. He had been by her side since the day he reclaimed her for England. However, he seemed unforgiving about her perceived treatment within the palace. He must have imagined her flitting from bed to bed. His dreams were a myth. She had merely been a student in the art of gratification.

"Let us not speak of the past." In truth, most of what she learned, she practiced on him. Recalling all the techniques she'd learned at the harem to please a man, she smiled. Queen Victoria was pleased with the secrets gained from Laurel's skill.

"So, who are the guests at the Embassy soiree this evening?" Aaron was barely audible. He strapped on his body modification. He lost his right arm during the Crimean War, and now a mechanical appendage rested in its place.

"Count Pierre Jean Claude, Commodore Emory Pembrooke, and newly appointed Inspector Raven Clarke of the Americas will all be in attendance." The mechanism drew her eye. His automaton was quite fascinating with its small clicks and whirs.

"Are you expecting General Tolstoy?" He flexed his gloved fingers before tightening the leather strap across his chest.

The mechanical gears seemed unnoticeable among the shiny brass parts and copper wires running across the interior of the gadget towards his shoulder. At the junction where his socket should be, a glass globe rested against his skin. Even smaller metal threads ran towards a miniature platform, on which sat a diamond the size of a pence. A doctor, who specialized in clockwork mechanisms and thermal conductivity, built the entire arm. Science had come far since the war. Many soldiers possessed body modifications, some better than their originals. Laurel knew Aaron was among a handful of lucky survivors who benefited from the latest clockwork expertise.

"No, the General will not be joining us." She preferred that the general didn't show as far as Laurel was concerned. She held no love for the nations in The Holy Alliance - Austria, Russia, and Prussia. She still was unable to forgive them and their war for the death of her husband.

"I look forward to Molly playing the pianoforte," he shrugged into his jacket.

"I turned her out," she winced and averted her eyes from his stare. Laurel dreaded telling him she released the Irish girl. Aaron spent a large amount of time with Molly Flannigan, and Laurel knew he had a soft spot for the courtesan from Dublin.

"Whatever for, my girl? Were you jealous? You know you are my favorite," he said with a wink, but the jest didn't quite reach his green eyes.

"I am not jealous." It was true; there was no room in her heart for Aaron, yet. "I caught her using Dover's powder. I just prefer the addicts stick to the opium dens, in the Crimson Lantern Ward. Molly was not getting the results needed for the Embassy trade. I'm willing to remove one girl, as opposed to losing them all." Laurel put on a brave face, not wanting Aaron to see her distrust and pass judgment. Turning Molly out had taken every ounce of her willpower. She had yet to tell the other girls.

Molly was a member of Laurel's inner circle. Even Aaron did not know all her secrets. When Laurel's father bartered her freedom for a title, Laurel knew she would need to make her own allies and find those like her. Those with magic. Molly, Fatima, and Victoria had been her closest confidants. She called them her tea girls, those hand-selected by Laurel, loyal only to her. When Fatima reported Molly's use of the opiate, known as Dover's powder, Molly left Laurel no choice. She couldn't afford Molly spilling secrets to Aaron or anyone else about Laurel's private teas. There was nothing to do now but suffer the consequences.

"Understandable. You don't want her sort, bringing down the empire." He shrugged matter-of-factly. "I'll see you downstairs." The door closed behind him with a hard click.

Laurel rose from the carved mahogany bed. The sapphire damask covers fell to her Persian rug. She walked to her extensive wardrobe, embellished with the same intricate heart pattern as her headboard, to dress for the evening.

Dark dresses of every fabric, season, and style nearly burst forth when she opened the door. Despite the brilliant jewel tones in her room, her wardrobe was not so colorful. There was no need for color. Laurel's bold manner and bawdy talk served her better when uncovering secrets for her queen.

Spies did not require daring tints, merely success. Laurel was nothing if not successful. She built this brothel, financed by the queen herself, and was more victorious than Secret Intelligence at furrowing out the misdeeds of Britain's enemies, particularly The Alliance.

Laurel picked bright scarlet pantaloons with wide black stripes to match her black chemisette. She fastened her dark stockings with garters, before artfully arranging her blond hair atop her head. The look was severe but pretty to the common eye.

Laurel wore a black lace bodice, to go over her chemisette. She tightened her heavy crimson corset over the bodice. While not the typical fashion, the corset served to titillate men and acted as body armor. A chain maille lattice was hidden within each silk panel of the rigid bone stays. The maille was heavy but worth the weight to protect the vital organs.

She finished her appearance with a heavy velvet skirt and boots. Beneath her skirt, she strapped a knife on a holster immediately below the garters. She always prepared for the unexpected.

Laurel placed tiny black opals in her ears, both pierced at the palace. She enhanced her brown eyes with kohl and pinched her cheeks. She bit her lip to brighten them before applying a tinted balm, giving a slight shine to her crimson lips.

Laurel turned to consider herself in the mirror. She was an image of dark among a sea of ruby and sapphire. She turned to the wardrobe and carefully unlocked a safe hidden in the back. She took out a dark velvet bag. Inside laid the jewel inspiring the room's design. The Sultan gave the gift to her, upon her departure, and told her it was from an admirer. The stone was crimson with cobalt veins, the size of her palm, and glowed brightly with an inner light. As always, the stone was warm within her hands, giving her a peculiar comfort. Laurel dare not resist rubbing the stone against her cheek, the action unconsciously bringing forth memories of love, laughter, and heartache. Her chest tightened and a tiny tear fell unbidden, making the gem seemingly sparkle. A small part of her knew the stone would always be with her, it was her heart.

Before heading downstairs she penned a note to Sir John Brown, private military counselor to the queen.

Sir B,

New Girls have arrived from America and Nippon. STOP.

Alliance continues to patronize the Horizontal. STOP.
Advise on next steps. STOP

~Lady G

* * *

AARON COULDN'T BELIEVE Laurel had let Molly go. He should go check on the girl to make sure Molly hadn't gone too far off the rails. Laurel seemed sure Molly wouldn't work out with the Dover's powder.

"Damn it all to hell." He muttered under his breath. Aaron certainly couldn't reveal he had been the one providing it. Given Laurel's profession, how could she be such a prude?

He made his way along the hallway, his boots clicked along the mahogany floorboards. Once he reached the stairwell, he surveyed what Laurel referred to as her parlor. He didn't have much time to track Molly down and get back to The Horizontal. He needed Molly back here to find out what Laurel was planning behind closed doors.

CHAPTER TWO

Inspector Raven Clarke perused the brothel, better known as 'The Great Britain Horizontal.' The scents among the guests were an assault on his sensitive nose. Liquor, tobacco, and opium filled his nostrils and sex filtering from above seemed to permeate the air. And that was just the humans. He chose a chair in the corner next to the fireplace, yet facing toward the room, particularly the open marble staircase leading to the second-level rooms.

William Seward would be impressed. Who would have thought beneath all the fluff and flounce, lay hardened spies? Seward informed Raven of the entire goings-on within the Global City. Raven looked to the Creole woman, Dominique Augustine, whom he'd escorted on the Atlantic crossing. She was in deep conversation with Count Jean Claude. Dominique was a true beauty. Light cinnamon skin and dark luminous eyes, along with her full mouth, would lead any man to bare his soul and secrets. Those secrets were most important to Seward and President Johnson. Allies were critical to America before deciding to intervene with New Archangel.

Raven was here to meet his contact, Lady Laurel Gunn. The woman had yet to make an appearance, not that Raven minded. Her tardiness gave him the time he needed to appear settled.

He kept an eye on the guard at the door. A man named Omar was the largest butler he'd ever seen. Raven was uncertain if the butler knew the duties, but he wore the suit. However, the long half-moon blade, hanging below his jacket, ruined the effect.

A hush filled the room.

Raven returned his focus to the stairs.

Lady Gunn finally deemed her guests worthy of her presence. She was quite the vision with her blond hair and dark eyes. She was exactly as she appeared, a hardened woman of business. Of course, Raven knew the secrets beneath this elaborate façade. The short missive Queen Victoria sent President Johnson regarding where a "chap of freedom, will find the finest conclusion" was unmistakable. He wasn't sure if even those in power knew besides a brothel used to gather secrets, the secrets might have been gathered by magickal means.

Raven listened to her conversation.

She made her way through the room.

"*Gluten Abend, Herr Gottschalk,*" she said to a Prussian man seated with a Japanese girl.

"*Oh, hallo, Frau Gunn. Wie geht ist Ihnen?*" He responded.

"*Ach ja, ganz gut, und Ihnen?*" She asked.

"*Danke, gut.*" The man laughed heartily, before pulling the geisha upon his lap.

"You're welcome," Laurel returned to English and smiled at the Prussian. She fulfilled her obligations to her patrons, and turned towards Raven with purpose, erasing any emotions from her features. She seemed to glide across the expansive marble floor, her movement alone made him doubt her humanity.

"Hello, I'm Lady Laurel Gunn and you are?" Her voice trailed off.

"Inspector Raven Clarke of New Archangel, madam." He rose to clasp her outstretched hand. Once he possessed her wrist, he raised and turned it, before pressing his lips to the sensitive skin. The scent of her was unlike anything he'd smelled before - brimstone and tears. He shivered.

"Inspector," her eyes widened, "such intimate behavior." She tried to pull her hand away.

"Is your establishment not about intimacy?" Raven held her hand. He placed his own on top and bowed his head closer to hers. He needed to know what kind of creature she was. Could he ruffle her perfectly smoothed feathers?

"The Great British Horizontal is about servicing the good men of

Great Britain, and her newfound allies. I do not believe we have allegiance to New Archangel." Laurel lowered her dark gaze.

"Not yet, but I believe we could become the best of allies, sharing our most private secrets." He whispered in her ear before he released her hand.

"We shall see, Inspector Clarke," her tone turned chilly.

"So formal! Call me Raven. We shall get to know one another well, I assure you." He smiled wickedly at her before patting her backside. How would the formal lady respond to his sinful behavior and what would she reveal?

* * *

It took every ounce of will she possessed not to slap his smiling face! Laurel was incredulous. It took all her willpower not to respond. He spanked her bottom, in front of all her girls, in front of Aaron! Laurel was a lady and dared not create a scene. She couldn't afford the risk. And, to think she felt sorry for him because of his eye patch.

Instead, she reached her hand around and grasped his hand, holding it. She applied pressure between his thumb and index finger until he winced.

"How we get to know each other, Inspector Clarke, will be on my terms, not yours." Besides causing him pain, her touch allowed her to see a human's demise. Raven Clarke was a blank slate which meant he was not human. It was one of the reasons she surrounded herself with fae. Her mother once told her 'Like cannot see like'.

"As much as I enjoy your lovely touch, I'd like my hand back." A silken thread of threat in his voice implied he might not be as subtle as she required.

"You Americans are so testy." Laurel released his hand, not wanting to waggle the tongues in the room.

Aaron was already eyeing her. She was fond of Aaron, but his level of protectiveness for her, in the business they were in, could get them both killed.

"Well, ma'am, I consider myself an Archangelist," he stated.

"Shh." She pressed her fingers to his lips.

Inspector Clarke opened his mouth, and she quickly removed her hand before allowing him to act inappropriately toward her.

"Let us sit." She motioned to the settee.

Once they were both seated, she turned her attention to him. "Inspector, your arrival to the Global City has already created rumors. You do not need to put a target on your back. If anyone asks, you are an American." She lowered her voice, being by design reserved.

"Ma'am, it would seem to me this place is enough of a target, with spies around every corner."

"Oh, sir, your assumptions are very mistaken," she assured him. There were spies for the crown, moles for The Holy Alliance, and of course the agents of the Veil to make sure all their cretinous rules were obeyed.

He raised the eyebrow over his patch, an obvious question.

"As you may have noticed I have women here from nearly every land," she explained.

He nodded.

"The Prussian and Russian women are not spies, nor are the French. This is by design. Victoria herself must approve of the women involved in the Embassy trade. Only the queen and I know the identity of the girls undercover." Laurel placed her hand on his knee, giving an appearance of familiarity.

"What about your business partner, Lieutenant Aaron March?" he asked, moving her hand up to his thigh, closer to his groin.

"Aaron knows only of the girls from the United Kingdom. He will now have to find a replacement for one, as I turned out his latest." Despite her disapproval of Inspector Clarke's intimate displays towards her person, she did need to gather intelligence. Perhaps she was sharing more information than was proper?

"How do you know the Veil isn't spying on you?"

"You are very astute, aren't you Inspector?"

He smiled at her compliment.

"The very reason Queen Victoria invited you and Miss Augustine was to help with ferreting out any human double agents."

"You want us to spy for you?" He sounded incredulous.

"Is information gathering not beneficial for both countries?" She ran her hand along his jaw.

"I suppose it is. But I'm more concerned about what is beneficial to Archangel and its inhabitants."

To keep his radicalism under control and satisfy her curiosity she changed the subject. "May I ask what happened?" Laurel's fingertip touched the strap tying the patch to his head.

He grasped her wrist.

She immediately lowered her hands and gaze to her lap, chiding herself inwardly for speaking without thinking.

"Civil War. Bayonet." His voice was curt.

"I am so sorry." The flood of sympathy she held when she first saw him came rushing back. She lifted her face.

"I don't need your pity, Miss Gunn." He seated himself further away from her.

"Misses," she corrected him.

"I beg your pardon?"

At his look of bewilderment, she covered her mouth and bit her lip to keep the laughter from bubbling forth. "I'm a widow. My husband died during the Crimean War. He too was an American, from Boston actually, a doctor, a lovely man." Laurel knew she was rambling; talking faster than her brain formed words. Her sorrow nearly overtook her fine-tuned control. *No Tears. Do not cry.* Twelve long years had passed, and grief still hung like an anchor around her neck.

"I had no idea." His hoarse whisper broke her cloud of gloom. "Is his death why you do this?"

"The killing of my husband is part of it." Laurel could not very well tell him within the toils of the Embassy trade, that she had found a sense of family. Her mother died in India and her own father had traded her freedom for land and a title. Her new friends gave her an unexpected strength and power which helped mask the deep grief of isolation.

* * *

THE CLEAVER WAITED. He could wait all night if necessary. Laurel Gunn had ruined Constantinople. Her house of ill repute sat right in the heart of commerce and within a stone's throw of the Embassy. His next victim would send a message that such trade would no longer be tolerated within the global city.

He waited in the shadows for his victim to appear. He had watched her enter 'The Great Britain Horizontal' through the side door, and in the alley upon her exit, she would meet her demise. He would, of course, move the corpse to the front of the establishment where patrons left the building after their night of sin.

The Cleaver put his fingers to his left temple, fighting with the warring voice inside him, the little sway, which warned Laurel did not deserve this. She was not like the other whores in the atrocious house. She was stronger, and despite the seriousness of the situation, she never cried, not once in the time he'd watched her. She would cry tears for him tonight.

"No!" He shouted to a moonless sky. He must fulfill his duty. His master needed him to do this. Disappointing Master was not an option. He would only suffer. Perhaps Laurel will fall ill with worry, for her girls. Maybe then, the establishment would close and he could be normal.

No, his dreams would never happen, not until he fulfilled his duty. He knew no peace in the depths of his soul. His lack of soul was the reason Master had chosen him. Only he performed the necessary violence without suffering a backlash of nightmares.

The immorality of his victims reminded him of his whore mother, who had given him away without a thought. Moreover, his father was a brutal and harsh man, unable to forgive anyone, including himself, for his transgressions.

He would do his task, and perform gladly, for his work was an example of punishment. He would mete out justice for those heathens who did not heed the warnings of the Holy Alliance and sought their own lustful pleasure.

The dancing girl exited the side door as he anticipated. He silently slithered behind her, snatching her with his left arm.

The dark-haired exotic dancer let out a short-lived scream.

He sliced her throat.

The blood flowed from her like a fountain, and she collapsed against him.

He dragged her remains towards the front of the whorehouse. He planned to perform the ritual and display her but was interrupted.

Little clicks, like claws on pavement, came from behind.

The Cleaver stole a glance down the alley. A shadowed devil appeared, ready to claim his soul. The demon ran from the lamplight towards him. No time for rituals, he had to leave. Now!

He dropped the girl and ran from his pursuer. He rounded the corner, but the cobbles and buildings were flooded with gaslight. He ran past the front of the brothel turning down the next alley. He needed to hide back in the shadows. No one must see him.

He turned into an even darker cross alley. He finally noticed the beady red eyes looking at him. Well hell! Bad enough he was nearly caught, now he would have to battle the scavenging beasts of the dark. He was not worried. They had no idea who they were dealing with. He raised his cleaver, prepared to slaughter them all.

CHAPTER THREE

*D*r. Benjamin Gunn awoke, reclining in his dental chair, with his chest wide open and a human heart in his bloody hand. His head pounded with the precision of a metronome.

"Dr. Gunn, sir, you passed out again." Moody hovered inches above him, concern etched onto his dark features.

Ben's glance took in his surroundings. At least he was still in his laboratory in Constantinople. He started to rise from the chair.

Moody held up his hand. "A moment."

"I need to wash up."

"You'll want to close up first." Moody nodded to Ben's wide-open chest.

Ben didn't have the time, "Damn it. Will you, Moody?" Ben placed the heart on the steel table next to him.

"But of course, sir." Moody proceeded to use his magic to seal Ben's chest. Once complete, the only reminder of the magic was a reddish-blue scar from his collarbone to his sternum.

"Thanks." Ben made his way to the small sink in the corner of the room. He methodically washed his hands, using the lye soap. The smell should bother him, but he was unaware. What did trouble him was his lack of memory.

"Did you see Missus Gunn?" Moody asked.

"No… I…don't recall."

"That's new." Moody looked at the heart on the table. "Human?"

"Yes."

"Where did you get it?"

"I wish I knew." Ben dried his hands. He rubbed his temples, trying to will his headache away and remember the events of the night. "I remember… I was going to enter the brothel, confront Laurel and this damnable thing she's been doing but I—" he trailed off.

"Don't worry sir. I'm sure it'll all come back to you."

"That's what I'm afraid of." Ben tried to put jumbled pieces together in his mind, but pain shot through his skull, preventing further exploration. He looked at the heart on the table. What horrible act had he committed? When the beast was in control, he never could remember a blasted thing.

"We'd better get this cleaned up, sir." Moody's voice broke through his nightmarish visions.

"Yes." Ben grabbed the formaldehyde and a sterile jar large enough to hold the heart. He poured enough liquid to submerge the organ. Once he sealed the jar, he placed the glass container among the many other specimens in his collection. Ben sprayed the table with vinegar to clear away the blood and the smell. He would find a way to make his own clockwork heart work efficiently. He'd already gotten the vulcanized rubber to flex more like actual valves and the thin brass held its shape better than the previous copper box.

"Did you get more?" Ben asked Moody.

"Of course," Moody responded, before emptying a black velvet bag on the table.

Diamonds spread across the dark metal like stars tumbling from the sky, assorted sizes and colors.

"These are excellent." Ben lifted the larger ones to inspect the fine angles of the stones. He gauged which stones would best work for thermal conductivity.

"Miss Laurel has the stone which would work best," Moody responded sharply, abandoning any pretense. Ben cautiously took a step back.

"I can't go to her Moody. Don't argue with me, not about this." His hands clenched. He worried about her every minute. A woman like Laurel shouldn't be in one of the most dangerous areas of the city. It was packed with desperate people, and too few of them were any good. Was it his death that had led her to the life she now lived? If only he'd been there to protect her, shelter her.

He lifted his fists to his forehead and barely kept himself from pounding them into his skull. Maybe if she'd never met him she wouldn't have been forced into a life of hell.

"Perhaps if you quit tinkering with your beating brass box, you will cease having lapses and burning through the stones." He and Moody arrived in the Global City over a year ago, and Ben had been shaken to find out Laurel was in Constantinople and running the renowned whorehouse.

A few months ago, while working in the political arena of the city, Ben was driven, through his own aimless wandering, to her very doorstep. He stopped to find his wife kissing a man outside the establishment. As he'd struggled not to scream at her, he remembered he was a monster. After glimpsing his wife with another, he'd watched from a distance, afraid to scare her with the knowledge of his existence.

"Perhaps, but even you know my heart doesn't work properly," Ben said. Though Moody was more powerful than Ben, he'd seemed content to take on a servant role since Ben awoke from his ordeal. Ben never questioned the balance of power in their relationship until now.

"You cannot avoid her forever." Moody's stare was blank despite the sensitive topic.

Ben knew he was right. The day would come when Laurel would find out he still lived. She would feel betrayed.

* * *

THE SCREAM PERMEATED the hallways until the sound finally echoed off the walls of the sitting room.

Laurel looked up.

The sound came from the kitchens.

She turned her head swiftly to check the entrance but Omar was already gone from his post to investigate.

Inspector Raven quickly stood and walked away from the settee, where he had been quietly speaking with Dominique.

"Relax gentlemen." Laurel rose calmly, then smoothed her skirts casually with one hand. "I'm sure it is nothing. Libby, my cook, likely saw a spider. She has such a flair for the dramatic."

Nothing was further from the truth. Raised in Whitechapel, Libby was a practical and steadfast girl.

Laurel requested Libby from her father's estate. Laurel's newly titled father and his fresh estate could afford to release a few servants when he'd done little else to help her.

As Laurel followed Inspector Raven down the narrow corridor, the mumblings of the kitchen staff grew louder as they drew near. The staff parted, like the Red Sea for Moses, when she approached, clearing her way to the side door.

Outside Omar held a sobbing Libby against him, comforting her.

At Libby's feet contrasting against the dirty dark cobble lay Fatima, who danced early this evening, now lay motionless.

Fatima's shalwar in robin's egg blue was stained with her blood. Her throat had been slit and her heart ripped from her chest.

A few of the local fauna had clearly torn her flesh as well.

"Fatima!" Laurel rushed forward and fell to her knees next to her friend. Even though she knew Fatima was gone, she needed to touch her one last time. "Fetch me a blanket!" She barked over her shoulder. Laurel lowered her face down to Fatima's, kissing her cooling cheek. Her hands closed Fatima's eyelids. *Do not cry.*

"The Cleaver." Omar handed her a woolen blanket.

Laurel gave a hollow laugh. What good was being one of the fae's most powerful creatures if she could not protect those she loved.

Omar was as vocal now as the day she met him.

Voices hummed around her, Laurel listened to distract herself from losing control.

"Who is this Cleaver?" the Inspector asked.

"The Cleaver is a dastardly fellow. Been killing in the city for nearly, what? Three months, Lovey?" Aaron spoke from the kitchen doorway.

"At least," Laurel choked. "This is the first heart to go missing. Are you sure it is him?" she asked, nodding to Fatima's now covered chest.

Aaron and Raven continued speaking.

Laurel tried to stay composed. She wanted to banish them all from her friend and mourn in private, not in front of those who knew nothing of her relationship with Fatima. She dared not reveal the enormousness of this loss anywhere but in the privacy of her own rooms.

"Indeed," Aaron agreed.

"Is he a cannibal?" asked Raven.

"That would be those buggers," Aaron nodded to the head lying near Omar's bloodied blade.

"What is that?" Raven asked.

"That, my simple American, is a dirty dodo. Sailors brought them from the New World. Normally, the dodos eat refuse but occasionally dine on carrion. The meat-eaters get bloody big. The bird over there," Aaron referenced the willow white feathers against the cobblestones, "looks almost four feet. I say, nice kill, Omar." Aaron murmured in approval.

"We can't leave her here," Laurel spoke with calm, despite the emotions choking her. She couldn't stop staring at the blood on the blanket around Fatima's chest, the same starburst pattern she'd seen before. The idea of the dodos dining on her friend's dead body turned Laurel's stomach.

"Of course not," Aaron replied. "Omar, my good man, could you bring Fatima to the wine cellar. We'll burn the side table once we've made arrangements."

"Her throat was slit. Don't you think we should investigate?" asked Inspector Clarke.

"I'd say it's obvious how she died, Inspector. I'm not sure how they deduce things across the pond, but here we tend to go with what we see. We don't have constables in this part of the city." Aaron's expression was one of aggrieved patience.

"Not everything is what it seems," replied Raven.

"You Americans are a bloody superstitious lot."

"Enough!" Laurel had as much as she could take with their 'pissing match,' as Ben would've called it. They stood there arguing over the corpse of one of her dearest friends as if Fatima's life was meaningless. She rose to her feet, taking control.

"Sorry, Lovey, what would you like to do?"

"I think an autopsy is in order," interjected the Inspector.

"I think you are not my Lovey." Aaron crossed his arms.

"Can someone perform an autopsy?" Laurel asked, certain she had all the answers. To ensure what happened to Fatima was due to the Cleaver and not related to the Embassy or The Horizontal.

"I don't believe we want to call a doctor from the Embassy." Aaron shrugged half-heartedly at her.

"What about the law?" Raven asked.

"Lieutenant Aaron March is correct. We are in the neutral district where all laws are subject to the Embassy," agreed Laurel.

"I will investigate and I'll find a doctor to perform the autopsy,"

Inspector Raven spoke in a tone filled with importance.

"Good luck chap, you'll need the Embassy's approval." Aaron leaned against the brick wall.

"I'm a member of the Embassy," Raven approached Aaron.

"As am I." Aaron met him halfway and their boots touched.

"Why do we need to involve them? It'll be bad for business." While a murder would hinder people coming to the Horizontal, Laurel bit the inside of her cheek to keep from crying out. She was fighting her grief and couldn't be concerned with trying to prevent a duel off the side of her kitchen. Dealing with these overgrown boys was trying her last nerve.

"Suggestions, Lady Gunn?" Raven ground out between clenched teeth, never looking at her.

"Let Inspector Clarke investigate. I'm sure, as Omar suggested, the Cleaver is the culprit, but I'd like to keep this crime secret. Can you be discreet, Inspector?"

"But of course, ma'am." Raven finally broke his staring contest to look at her.

"Aaron?" she pleaded.

Her lover turned to her, only because she'd used his given name, she was sure.

"I'll be watching you, Inspector." Aaron pivoted on his heel to leave.

"What a pompous ass," Raven muttered under his breath.

"Inspector, please refrain from calling my partner by anything other than his title."

"Yes, Lady Laurel," he leaned toward her and lowered his voice to just above a whisper.

"Omar, please bring Fatima to the wine cellar as Lieutenant March suggested. Inspector, I suggest you go find a doctor." Laurel said briskly, before turning to find solace in the quiet of her room.

CHAPTER FOUR

Raven adjusted his seating in the "Jumbo" as the natives called the giant steam-powered elephants. The cushion slid along the wood bench, forcing him to grip the velvet rope above his head. The smell of grease and metal filled his nostrils.

For a modern marvel, there were a few kinks to work out. The brass pachyderms were far more impressive than some of the bicycles he'd seen about the city. The Jumbo's legs lowered using hydraulics. Once Raven was safe inside the red velvet-lined howdah, the hydraulics raised him and the lumbering beast from the ground.

He watched as the mahout, dressed in black from head to toe, filled the mouth of the metal beast with wood and oil, before inserting a torch to ignite the fire. The spring on the elephant's mouth snapped shut, and the rider quickly climbed behind the brass head in a leather seat. A seat that looked more comfortable than the gilded cage Raven was seated upon.

The eyes of the brass animal glowed orange like the embers of a fire. Steam rose out of its trunk, creating an ear-piercing whistle. Raven covered his sensitive ears, ineffectively blocking out the noise. The beast's head was akin to a tea kettle. Hadn't these people heard of horses? The trip to find a doctor was far too slow and unfamiliar.

Raven was still adjusting to the movements of his awkward trans-portation when the mechanical beast finally stopped. Between the whistle of the Jumbo and the smell of the mechanics, he couldn't use his powers of detection. Raven decided he would walk back to The Horizontal with the doctor, rather than suffer the discomforts of something easily replaced by a carriage.

The physician's office was down the street from the political powerhouse of the Embassy and ran parallel to the alley where Fatima, the dancer, had been killed.

Interesting.

Raven rapped on the door before him, the brass knocker depicted two snakes wound around a winged staff, indicating a physician resided within.

"May I help you?" A lean, young man with dark hair and olive skin answered the door. He was dressed all in black leather and his ink-colored hair covered his eyes.

"I'm here to see the doctor?"

"The doctor is not seeing new patients," the servant lifted his face and golden eyes moved in a sweeping motion from the cowboy hat resting on Raven's head to his polished black boots as if determining worthiness. Those eyes were damn disturbing and reminded Raven of dancing fire.

"I'm not here as a patient," Raven corrected.

The man arched a brow before attempting to close the door.

Raven placed his foot in the entrance.

"Who is it, Moody?" Raven heard a voice ask from beyond the oak barrier his foot held.

"A persistent stranger, Da--Doctor."

The door opened wider and the servant stepped away. Raven assessed the new stranger before him. He had dark reddish-brown hair and dark green eyes. His gray suit was finely tailored and he had a white cravat tied around his neck, tucked into a matching gray vest. All the buttons on his vest were done up but the jacket remained loose as if tossed on. Unlike his suit, his shoes were worn and appeared damp with fresh sediment on them. He held an ornate cane in his right hand, and though the walking stick rested on the tiled floor, the man appeared not to bear weight on it.

"Are you the doctor?" Raven asked.

"I am."

"I'm here to see you about a murder at the Great British Horizontal."

* * *

"WHO'S BEEN KILLED?" Ben's gut clenched and his clockwork heart omitted a pump, the whirring of his box noticeable to those in the room. He steadied himself against his walking stick. His first concern was Laurel. Had she been harmed?

"Fatima. She was one of the veiled dancers," the man answered.

Ben's sigh was audible, he knew, and he uttered a soft curse. "Come in Mister...I'm sorry, I don't believe Moody gave me your name."

"Inspector Raven Clarke was recently transported from America. Like you, I believe?"

"Not newly, but originally. Where do you hail from, sir?" It was odd to have an American in Constantinople, there seemed to be more Europeans mulling about.

"The Russian American settlement."

"By the Canadian Yukon?" Ben fetched his coat off the hook, along with his gray derby. "Archangel territory?" He paused looking this man over with a hard look.

"Yes, you've heard of it?" The inspector raised a brow.

"My family nearly settled there." Ben left it at that. No sense in giving the man more ammunition than he needed. He wasn't certain whether this man was a friend or foe.

"Will you help me investigate this death?"

"Of course, as a physician, I'm sworn to help the living. However, the least I can do is assist the dead in search of justice." Although his main concern was to see Laurel safe.

"Sir," Moody grabbed Ben's arm, "Are you sure you should go to the brothel?"

"What if Laurel is in danger? I have to help her," Ben whispered low hoping the Inspector couldn't hear.

Moody merely nodded his agreement.

As he and Raven left his house and exited toward the alley, the Inspector asked the tell-all question. "I'm sorry, doctor; I didn't get your name?"

"Dr. Benjamin Gunn," he answered. There was no avoiding it, or any consequences coming from this night.

"Any relation to Lady Laurel Gunn?"

He didn't even try to lie. The truth would eventually be revealed. "She's my wife."

* * *

LAUREL'S quiet mourning was broken by a knock on the door.

"Come in." Laurel suspected she must look a fright with her red eyes and nose, but she did not care.

"Lady, the Inspector collected a doctor," Omar announced as he stood beneath the threshold of her doorway.

"Very well," she ground out. "Let me know when the examination of Fatima is complete and if our suspicions regarding the Cleaver are confirmed." She wanted solitude.

"Laurel, you must come below."

She turned at Omar's informal use of her name. He'd never called her by her given name, not since he'd taken her to the palace.

"What's wrong?" she asked.

"The doctor is…well…best you see." Omar's voice was broken, but his gaze was firm.

Laurel rose from her Sleepy Hollow rocker and set her tea on the russet mahogany sideboard. She grasped the gas lantern off its curved hinge and followed Omar to the cellar.

The house was hushed. The events of the evening set an eerie silence in the air.

They moved down the stairs, perhaps more quiet than usual.

Laurel walked towards the courtyard and beyond to where Fatima lay in the cool wine cellar.

"No, ma'am, the Inspector and doctor are waiting in the parlor."

Laurel halted. "Whatever for?"

"As I said earlier, you'll want to meet the doctor for yourself." He directed her back to the main house.

"Omar, you are seriously testing my patience." Her brows drew together in an agonized expression.

The Inspector had probably chosen one of those bloated windbags whose mere presence in her home brought the doctor to apoplexy.

"My apologies, my lady."

"Of all the nonsense," she mumbled under her breath. She had an edgy twitchy feeling upon seeing the outline of the physician and rushed towards the stairs not thinking or caring about the consequences.

Before they reached the parlor, Laurel stopped. Shivers ran along her skin, and the familiar odor of sandalwood filled her nose. Her knees nearly buckled and Omar, seeming to sense her weakness, held her arm beneath her elbow, while resting the other on her back.

"It will be alright, my lady," his low baritone voice did little to calm her weary composure. What was wrong with her?

She saw Raven at the parlor entrance, apparently pleased, like a cat rewarding her with a mouse. As much as she would like to find Fatima's killer, the girl's death wasn't what unsettled her.

When she rounded the column, she knew why she shook uncontrollably and her heart raced. He stood facing away from her but she'd recognize the stance of her husband anywhere.

"Ben?" She reacted on instinct. Raw need propelled her towards him.

He turned. His face was harsh looking, like weathered stone left out in the elements, tough yet still handsome. His green eyes seemed to probe her for questions. "Yes?"

Laurel slapped him hard, the crack echoed across the marble tiles.

She shook her stinging hand.

She straightened and anchored her feet.

Her hand-print now a pink mark on his cheek held her gaze. She finally found her voice. "You bloody bastard, you're supposed to be dead!"

CHAPTER FIVE

Twelve years earlier Crimean War
Ottoman camp at Batoum

The smell of sulfur, metal, and ether filled the small medical tent. Doctor Benjamin Gunn worked on the Tunisian soldier strapped to his table. He carefully stitched the leg. When would the next supply wagon arrive at Batoum?

His inventory was running low and he was thankful he had an abundant case of ether because the drug was the only thing helping patients. Doctor Gunn's supply of penicillin was low. He'd resorted to medicating only those with signs of infection. The aspirin was gone, as well as the alcohol he'd used to sterilize his instruments. He frequently used the flame from gas lamps or the occasional candle to sterilize instruments and hoped for the best until his charges reached a proper medical facility.

The best was a nurse named Florence, who would see to the soldiers' proper recovery if Ben could get them to Renkioi Hospital. Until the supply lines were secure, the British wouldn't even consider transferring patients.

A feminine throat cleared behind him.

Ben turned to his English bride of almost a year.

"Will he be alright?" Laurel was the only good thing to come since the

United States Secretary of War, Jefferson Davis, sent him to this god-awful place.

"He'll be fine, although now I wonder about the use of stitching a simple wound from a bayonet." Ben removed his apron and looked at his wife. He rinsed his hands in the washbasin.

Laurel's golden blond hair was wrestling to break free from the severe hold at the nape of her neck. Her serviceable gown was the color of ash, much like the scorched earth outside, her fresh apron appearing stark against the unending destruction.

"You've always done fine work with a needle," her eyes perused his handiwork. "However, I question times when we refer to the slicing of a man's flesh as simple." She lifted her head, revealing the wetness gathering in her deep brown eyes.

Ben couldn't help but gather her in his arms, hoping to protect her from the horrors surrounding them. She shouldn't see this; no one should witness this level of blood, devastation, and death.

Laurel returned his embrace with such intensity of emotion, that it terrified him. She might be used to scarce conditions, being the daughter of a missionary, but this was more than any human should have to bear.

"Are you alright?" Ben pulled back and stared intently at her delicately carved face, searching for signs of illness.

"I'm fine, my heart," she reassured him, before kissing him on the lips and wriggling free.

Ben smiled at her term of endearment and let her have her way.

"Dr. Gunny do good work."

The couple turned to find Moody Jinn looking over the Tunisian soldier's stitches, a book dangling from his hand. Even if Laurel hadn't broken free, the child's comment would've surely dampened their embrace.

"You think so?" Laurel leaned down next to the boy, removing the book from his tiny fingers and setting the tome on a nearby folding chair. She continued mothering the boy, by taking a damp cloth and cleaning the ink smudges from his face. The two had been close since his wife rescued the boy from joining the cause of the Tunisian Army by rescuing him. She saved the money to buy material for her wedding gown; instead, she bought the child in lieu of a dress for their marriage. The boy had been like a younger brother at first, but lately, he'd taken to calling her "Mum".

Her father hadn't been pleased, but it was obvious Laurel hadn't given a hoot what her father thought. If she had, she wouldn't have married Ben in the first place.

"Thank you," Ben stated to the child.

"Welcome, sir."

"If you're going to use a title Moody, please call me doctor, the only sirs are knights from Laurel's country," Ben winked at his wife.

Laurel rolled her brown eyes and squeezed the child closer to her side. "You call him whatever you want, dearest."

* * *

"You, husband, are incorrigible." No sooner had the words left her mouth than the air was punctuated with gunfire.

She jumped as whistling noises increased outside the small tent, and balls whizzed by. The cracking of powder approached in the distance.

Ben moved the soldier and another patient from the opening of the tent together towards the back and placed a steel shield over their bodies.

They took cover underneath the gurneys.

The booms and bangs continued their assault outside the small haven they seemed to have created. The air thickened with sulfur and dust.

She couldn't seem to catch her breath. Her heartbeat was fast and she was tempted to greet death rather than stay trapped in this place. The moment so reminiscent of when her father would lock her in a trunk.

They lay huddled beneath the wounded waiting for the war to pass by. Ben's strong arms wrapped around her, and her own limbs entwined Moody.

She hoped the battle would spare them. Time moved slowly before the air finally cleared and the ringing in her ears stopped.

"Do you think it safe, Sir?" Moody's small voice whispered.

"You both remain here, I will see," he said.

Laurel reached out to her husband, grasping his hand, begging him silently not to leave. She didn't feel safe yet. An unseen force tingled along her spine, warning her.

"Laurel, it will be alright." Ben patted her hand before breaking her hold.

She listened to the small movements of her husband.

He checked on the patients, and secured items that had fallen over.

Her throat itched. She ached to call him back to her.

"Damn it," he cursed.

"What?" Laurel peered out of the makeshift shelter. What did Ben find amiss?

"The ether is missing." He pointed to where the bottles should be in the crate near the flap.

Laurel's sigh was audible.

Her husband glared at her.

"I'm sorry, Ben, but I would much rather live without medicine than you, or Moody, or one of your freshly repaired patients," she placed her hands on her hips. "Besides which, ether is explosive and could kill us all," Laurel was not about to feel guilty over her relief.

"I know, you're right, and I'm sorry," Ben started towards her.

A gunshot tore through the air, stopping Ben in his tracks.

"NO!" Laurel screamed in horror.

Crimson slowly spread in a sunburst pattern across his ivory linen shirt. Ben fell backward hitting the burned grass with a thud. *No Tears. Do not cry.*

Like lightning scattering through clouds, Laurel closed the distance towards her husband, not caring what lay in her path. She looked up to find Tunisian soldiers, bringing up the rear, running towards the tent.

"My husband has been shot! Do you have someone with you who has medical knowledge?"

They stared at her wordlessly, no comprehension on their faces.

"Moody, help me." She called out, checking Ben's neck for a pulse.

"What you need?" Moody moved to her side in silence.

"Laurel, take care…my love," Ben's hoarse and broken words were barely audible. The emerald light of his eyes, typically filled with humor, were hollow. His skin was starting to turn a bluish hue.

No Tears. Do not cry.

"Shhhh. Stay with me, my heart." Laurel smoothed the lines of worry on his brow. She pushed back his auburn hair and pressed closer to him.

"My heart…yours…do as you please," he closed his eyes.

"Ben! Ben! Open your eyes, don't you dare leave me!"

Ben's eyes remained shut.

"Mum, he's gone," Moody touched her arm.

"Do not dare speak like that!" In the year she'd known Moody, she'd never turned on him. But to lose Ben without warning, nothing. Her gift had given her no sign. Her grief unhinged her. Now she felt like a viper ready to strike. She needed to know. Laurel tore open his shirt, heedless to the buttons flying like small artillery around the tent.

She pulled her apron over her head and quickly soaked up the blood, so much blood. She placed her ear to his chest, unconcerned about appearances. She heard no breath and willed for his chest to rise beneath her willing touch.

"Please stay with me, my heart," she rested against his chest and waited. No sound. She had nothing. She married Ben to escape her over-bearing, missionary father. She did not intend to return to the man who would sell her to the highest bidder.

"Mum, you go with Omar here, he speaks English good."

Omar said nothing but grasped her arm tightly.

"Moody, I—" Laurel was numb, unable to vocalize her wishes.

"I will take care of."

Laurel stared at the boy she'd raised for a year. He appeared to grow significantly in a matter of minutes. Moody seemed removed from the nickname she'd given him. He was calm, older, wiser, and more powerful. If anyone could heal Ben, it might be Moody. Her relief was short-lived.

"Go now," Omar threw her forward.

"My husband," her voice cracked, and tears threatened to fall. She rigidly held her tears in check. Her father had reprimanded her at any sign of crying. *No Tears. Do Not Cry.*

"Dead," Omar pushed on her back with the hilt of his sword.

"I come find you when I fix," Moody shouted from the tent, growing smaller.

Omar dragged her away.

"Where are we going?" Her vision was clouded by unshed tears. The stifled cry of injustice suffocated her voice. Laurel stepped back and clutched at her chest, not truly believing what happened.

"Sultan's harem," Omar spoke behind her.

"Harem?" She twirled around to face him.

"Boy says you be safe there."

"You misunderstood; you need to take me to the Consulate." Laurel stood her ground. The Sultan's harem be damned.

"No. Harem." Omar drew his Damascus steel blade, emphasizing his position.

Laurel debated for two entire seconds about traveling with this large man down the road and decided better against it. She made a run back to the tent, Ben, and the life she knew.

She was about to shout at Moody when Omar snatched her about the waist and hit her in the back of the head with the hilt of his blade.

Before succumbing to darkness, Laurel wondered why life was cruel to take away her heart and send her to another man's harem.

CHAPTER SIX

Great Horizontal Brothel
1868

aurel waited for her husband to acknowledge her. How many nights had she silently cried to sleep mourning his death? Now he stood before her and rather than elation he was alive, she was angry. Angry at him for not seeking her out. Angry at the twist of fate for stealing her life from her. And angry at herself for stolen moments with Aaron. The Norns were cruel to throw Ben into her life so soon after Fatima was lost. Despite the tingling, her fingers itched to strike him

"I've missed you too, my heart." Despite her provocation, Ben's eyes scanned her for injuries.

She was startled at the concern in his polished jade eyes. It was the doctor in him. His worry had nothing to do with her personally, she reminded herself. Her blood-shot eyes and shaking hands probably prompted his perusal.

"Don't call me that. You've lost the right," she fumed at him.

Ben lowered his gaze from hers before speaking, "Where's the body?"

Typical of Ben, rather than dealing with the problem outright, he fell back on his duty. Had duty kept him away from her?

"Follow me." She struggled to keep her voice level as she led him along the corridor.

"How are you?" His voice hummed along her spine like pebbles rolling downhill, and she responded by increasing her stride across the tiles.

"Fine." Inside she felt nothing close to passable.

Her stomach churned.

Her heart strummed fast inside her ears, pounding hard, and she swore the thud was as audible as Ben's footsteps behind her.

"I'm sorry." His voice was barely a whisper beside her internal raging sea of emotion.

She pivoted on her heel quickly.

Ben ran right into her.

Immediately her hands clutched at his shoulders, to keep from falling backward.

Ben's arms lowered and encircled her waist, steadying her.

"What part do you apologize for Ben?" Laurel pushed him.

She took two steps back, away from his touch. She ran her hands along her sides and smoothed down her skirts. "Are you sorry I spent five years in a harem, learning the trade? Are you sorry my father would have disowned me if not for the queen bribing him with a title? Are you sorry I lie in another man's arms? Or perhaps you are merely sorry I no longer belong to you."

"All of those. I am sorry to have caused you such pain." His eyes had grown clear and his features thoughtful.

Laurel clasped her right wrist in her left hand to keep from reaching out to him. She remained still, though her fingers itched to touch the fine lines of his face and smooth away his concern.

"Damn you, Ben," she whispered. He didn't deserve any of her affection.

"Pardon?"

"There was pain. I was awash with it. I was beginning to find solace finally and now..." Now Fatima was dead, Molly was lost, and Victoria was living elsewhere. Once again, she was alone.

"Now?" he prompted.

"You stand before me and I'm uncertain how to proceed." She hung her head low, taking deep breaths. Laurel was still struggling for composure when his arms embraced her with a rock-steady shield.

She went rigid. If she relaxed, words would tumble from her mouth, like mortars finding their mark.

"Shh, my heart. Let me hold you. You may always find comfort and understanding in my arms."

"Ben?" Laurel bit her lip stopping her cry.

"It is a simple thing,". His arms wrapped around her. His hands were steady and calm.

Laurel clutched at his jacket lapels for fear she would sink. She was drowning in a river of emotion and memory, which threatened to carry her downstream away towards rocks, hard and immovable. Those same stones would likely kill her rather than protect her from the swift current.

Survival and the need to protect her heart gave her the strength to push against his chest, breaking the chain of his arms.

"Thank you for your concern Doctor Gunn, however, I will be quite fine I assure you." Laurel clenched her hands into fists and unclenched them, hoping to hide the trembling within her limbs.

"Laurel—" His green eyes begged her to stay.

She resisted his lure.

"This way please." She turned abruptly, and walked briskly down the hall, desperate to put distance between them.

They continued in silence towards the room where Fatima lay.

Once they arrived at the room, Laurel stood back by the door, guarding against intruders.

Ben removed the blanket from Fatima and Laurel exited the tiny room, telling herself Ben required freedom to analyze.

In the hall, she savored her freedom, having escaped close quarters with Ben as he examined Fatima. She was *so* focused on her breathing that she didn't hear approaching footsteps.

* * *

RAVEN'S long strides reached Laurel Gunn in a matter of minutes. She was leaning back against the wall, her long fingers pale against the limestone. She appeared to clutch the grooves along the wall. Her eyes were closed, and her head tilted slightly forward. She was taking deep breaths. Her chest strained against her corset.

"Are you alright?" He suspected witnessing her husband back from the dead upset her far more than Fatima's corpse.

"I'm fine." She rose and quickly appeared alert. Her action caused him to take a step back. She ran her hands along her skirt ironing the fabric.

"I'm sure you are." How did Laurel mingle in the emissary business without revealing any truths? Despite her red eyes and the scent of salt along her cheek, the woman before him was slowly gaining composure.

"What do you want, Inspector?" Any sign of feeling disappeared with each gesture.

"I wondered if the good doctor concluded anything." Raven witnessed her brief moment of weakness. He was sure she was not likely to forget it.

"I'm not certain, Inspector. Enter if you choose. I shall caution you, Benja –Dr. Gunn doesn't care for interruptions." Mrs. Gunn turned and walked away from him.

Raven hoped he hadn't made an enemy of Laurel Gunn. He rather liked her. She added a type of verbal sport he didn't share with other women. He had hoped to pull her away from her obvious lover, but a husband was a different matter.

Deciding not to knock, he pushed the door open and charged into the room. The average person would have jumped back startled at the least provocation.

"Can I help you?" Doctor Gunn remained focused on the task before him. He wore a spyglass contraption strapped to his head. He examined her right wrist.

"What have you discovered? "Raven inquired.

"Not much of anything, yet." The doctor's hands traveled the length of her arm. He applied subtle pressure. "Nothing appears broken. Looking at her wrists, it doesn't appear as if she fought her attacker."

"Was she drugged?" Raven took a step towards the table. He leaned towards the body inhaling any scent that might indicate Fatima's attacker.

"Don't move," the doctor growled at him.

Raven stopped mid-step, his foot coming down hard on the tiles. He gave the doctor a quizzical look.

"I don't need you in my space."

"What area in this room is yours?" Raven stretched his arm out.

"Don't be obtuse. You know very well I don't need you hovering behind me. Allow me the freedom to move and *inspect* after me. You may go down there by her feet." Doctor Gunn pointed to his right.

Raven crossed to investigate Fatima's sandals, "Doctor, why didn't you remove her sandals?"

"It wasn't relevant to her murder. Feel free to have at them; I've already examined her toes, inspector."

What a pompous jackass!

Dr. Gunn scrutinized the slice through the dancer's neck. "It appears her neck was cut from left to right. You can see here the cut deepens at this angle. This indicates the assailant was likely right-handed."

"I see you are right-handed, Doctor," Raven noted.

"As is most of the population," the doctor continued his examination, with no apparent regard to Raven's comment. "I wonder if…"

The doctor took a magnifying glass in his left hand and seemed to stare at the gaping wound in detail. He paused with a tweezer in his right hand.

"Damn it, nothing."

"You were hoping to find something, doctor?"

"Yes, possibly a fiber or hair to help your case."

Raven ignored Doctor Gunn and looked at Fatima's sandals. "You missed the evidence under her feet."

"I understood she was killed right outside the door of the establishment. Do you have reason to believe otherwise?"

"I believe in finding out where the sediment came from and discovering if the origins are relevant to her demise."

"Seems reasonable," the doctor replied and handed him a glass jar. "Use this."

"Rather large, but I shall make do." He pulled his *PAL RH36* knife from his boot and using the blunt side, scraped the small pebbles and dirt from the bottom of her footwear. "I'll leave you to our damsel then doctor."

"Yes, yes…move along." Doctor Gunn dismissed him.

* * *

BEN SIGHED ONCE the door snapped shut behind Inspector Clarke. He was afraid he would be discovered. After all, he was secretly searching for evidence of his own shame. He knew without detailed analysis he'd *awakened* with the heart from her body.

His initial glance at the open cavity told him the organ *had* rested within. He didn't see any signs of the organ being cut; terrifyingly, the organ appeared to have been ripped from the flesh.

Did he do that?

What was he capable of in those moments when he lost all memory?

Ben found no signs his beast within had perpetrated this crime. His discovery was of small significance when he possessed the girl's heart and was concerned he was involved in some manner in Fatima's demise.

Was he the Cleaver who haunted the Constantinople alleys killing young girls?

Bile rose in his throat at the suggestion. If so, he had come right to Laurel's doorstep.

Ben took a deep breath. He needed to discover more and take his knowledge to Moody. He trusted Moody to protect Laurel, even if he didn't trust himself.

* * *

"Too long a day, Lovey?" Aaron entered Laurel's room and reached to touch her hair.

"Long day is putting it mildly." Laurel ducked beneath his fingers and sidestepped him.

Aaron withdrew his hand. "Do you want to talk about it?"

She did want to talk about it, but she was not sure if Aaron was the person to confide in. On the other hand, Aaron was one of the few people who knew her history, much as she knew his own.

"I really would like to, if you don't mind?" she asked. With all her allies gone, he seemed as good a person to share her feelings with as any.

Aaron seated himself in her rocking chair. "My dear love, why on earth would I mind? Your husband does present a challenge. I imagine things will change between us. I certainly don't find the chap as annoying as that Raven fellow." Aaron smiled.

Laurel could not tell what his emotions were; he had always been able to guard his feelings. His calm facade was also one of the reasons she kept many of the crown's secrets to herself, along with the fact that his mother was Russian. His lineage made many in Victoria's counsel suspicious. Of course, she didn't suspect Aaron of treason, never that. He was a man who had risen through the social ranks, despite his less than noble birth. She and Aaron were kindred spirits. She believed the aristocracy would never truly accept them because they were not born into the fine breeding lines. Her nobility had come at a high cost, but the titles were important to her father.

"Start at the beginning, my dear," Aaron coaxed her.

"After we found Fatima, and Inspector Clarke returned with Be—Dr. —my husband, it was such a shock; truly I'm surprised I didn't expire on the spot." Laurel sat at her dressing table and removed the pins from her hair. There was no reason to treat this conversation differently from any other. If anything, remaining composed was essential.

"I would imagine seeing the man you believed dead would cause quite a distress. Tell me more about him."

"Ben is very much like me," she paused, cautious about what to reveal to this human. "He grew up with a modest family and traveled around." Laurel would never forget a single detail of Ben's background. The memories of Ben telling her about his family brought a hidden smile.

"His father is a missionary?"

"Not exactly…" Laurel intentionally left his parents' professions out. Leave it to Aaron to root out the details.

"What is their vocation then?"

"His parents are both performers."

"Theatre? Opera?"

"Circus," she whispered the single word, hoping Aaron wouldn't grab onto the information like a bone. Circus performers were considered for the masses, not the elite.

"Really? That is very unusual. However, did he end up as a physician?" He asked, trying to piece together a puzzle.

"His father swallows swords and eats fire. One time during the performance, his mother was burned. There was a doctor in the audience and the man treated Ben's mum. She wasn't badly injured, but the doctor's healing was enough to fascinate a ten-year-old Benjamin Gunn. His mother's influential family members helped Ben into a boarding school, from there he attended Edinburgh." The story of Ben's parents still fascinated her today. She had never met them, perhaps she would now. She was determined to discover what kind of creature her husband truly was. Laurel shook her head. Solving that mystery would have to wait until they determined who killed Fatima.

"And then he met and married lovely you." He leaned forward and gazed at her reflection.

Laurel nodded mutely. It wasn't exactly how she met her husband, but the story would do.

"Do you mind if I ask how he died?"

Laurel turned away from the mirror, struggling to maintain a blank canvas in the face of Aaron's morose question. She failed miserably.

"My dear, don't look at me as if I killed your prize puppy. You've never spoken of his death and I admit a morbid curiosity as to how a man rises from the grave."

She never once voiced how Ben had died. She did not care for the staff to apologize or speak of the unfairness of life. Laurel had to train her employees in stoicism. She could not set an example to the recruits if she was a puddle of emotion, recounting the demise of her beloved husband.

"Ben was shot in the heart," she clipped. The knowledge that her husband was alive made the words bearable.

"The heart you say? Are you certain?" He asked, rubbing his chin.

"Believe it or not Aaron, before I tended to men's needs, I tended their wounds on the battlefield." Her voice was laced with heat.

"Calm down, Lovey. Do you not wonder how a man without a heart walks among us?" Aaron said in a hushed breath.

"Is that your inner surgeon talking?" Laurel smiled. He reminded her of Ben, there was no mystery she was drawn to him.

"Of course, and I do wonder if your revived spouse has had some enhancements."

"Like a clockwork heart?"

"Exactly that."

"I'm not sure where Ben would come across such technology."

"Likely the same way I did."

"You were restored in a Prussian hospital by a very talented doctor."

"Perhaps Doctor Gunn benefited from the same advancements."

"Aaron, you know the only people with the skill for clockworks are the Prussians, and even they haven't advanced beyond the limb such as yours. If they had, there would be far more living people walking about." Laurel had never heard of a human possessing a clockwork heart, but she knew that her husband was not exactly human either.

The pins from her thick hair were scattered about her dresser. Laurel worried her lip, normally she would be removing her corset and readying herself for bed.

"It's alright Laurel. Do not fret." His kind words and the depth, with which he knew her, caused the maelstrom of emotions to break.

Laurel held the dam no more. She hung her head, swallowed hard, and bit back the tears.

Aaron quickly moved to her side. He turned her on the bench and knelt between her legs. Grasping her face between his hands, he said, "Laurel, my dear, you are not alone. Though your heart may be confused, mine is not. If I cannot be your lover, at least let me be your friend."

Aaron embraced her. She rested her head on his shoulder. Laurel let her grief win and surrendered to silent tears.

Do not cry!

She choked on the scream. If released Laurel would truly lose control and reveal more than her silent pain.

CHAPTER SEVEN

*A*aron's softened cock slid out of Molly. He missed her around The Horizontal. Her laughter tickled along his spine and her freckled face softened whenever she looked upon him.

"Aaron my love, I missed ye and our times together." Molly ran her foot along the back of his calf.

"I too, m'dear. Lord above knows I would see much more of you with Laurel's husband returned from the dead." He rolled off Molly, laying back to rest his head on his pillow.

"What!" Molly rose up on her elbows, turning towards him, the sheet twisting and baring a voluptuous breast with its rose peak to his satiated gaze.

"Oh yes, the news was quite a shock. You should have seen Omar's jaw drop. The single movement was the most expression anyone had seen on the man."

"Omar was always a mite stoic, he was." Molly concurred with him. "How did ye find out about the good doctor's return from the dead?"

"Fatima was killed outside The Horizontal by the Cleaver last evening," Aaron announced.

Molly's heart stopped. She could barely breathe and inhaled deeply, gulping in air.

"I'm sorry m'dear. I often forget she was your friend." Though his tone was soft the blow wasn't any less.

"Hardly," Molly gave a loud snort. "Fatima, being just a dancer, thought she was better than those who whored. Surprised, I am. A killing close to where I used to hang my knickers." She prayed she sounded nonchalant.

"Well, I imagine he was bound to arrive there sooner or later. The Cleaver being such a Puritan sort. I'll have to bring on extra security for the girls."

"What about your toff patrons?"

"They are not as much of a commodity as the spies, are they? Molly, m'dear, I worry about you out here in the world alone. Are you certain you cannot resist Dover's powder? I would see you return to The Horizontal." His voice was uneven as he spoke.

"Do you miss your own personal spy, Lieutenant?" Molly rolled over, pressing her breasts against his side.

"You know I miss you Molly-girl." He absently flicked her plump nipple with his index finger.

"Show me how much Aaron." Molly climbed astride him, ready for another go, and of course, Lieutenant Aaron March was not a man to shirk his duty.

* * *

THE CLEAVER FOLLOWED Molly Flannigan from the officer housing to the Red Lamp district. Molly made her home among the opium dens, bathhouses, and homeless guttersnipes. Even Laurel, the queen's whore, knew Molly was beyond redemption when she banished Miss Flannigan to this forgotten place.

The Cleaver slid back into the shadows with his prey under scrutiny.

Molly beckoned a bearded man from the night to meet her underneath a corner lamp.

He stalked.

She seemed to haggle with the man before removing coins from a hidden pocket in her bodice.

The bearded hawker handed her a small blue bottle before returning to the darkness.

The whore was obviously among friends. She jovially visited with the boys outside the bathhouse before making her way to Tom's Tavern. Molly was at the very end of the district where the cobble no longer existed and the roads turned to sand.

The wind pushed the sand against the sides of the buildings and down the street to engulf and purify the desecration all around. Even the desert threatened to banish these vagrants in this ghetto. It was a sign he did good work. His resolve stopped the quiver in his stomach. He had to kill Miss Molly Flannigan.

* * *

MOLLY WALKED on the narrow steps of the tavern to her room above. Discomfort tingled along her spine, reminding her of her grandmother's ghost stories and someone walking across her grave. She stopped suddenly, turning around. No one followed her. She shook her head, shaking off superstition and nonsense. Perhaps she should have stayed with Aaron.

She clutched the bottle she purchased tighter. Though Aaron had her best interests at heart, he had no idea how painful her memories were this time of year. She truly needed the syrup to help her sleep and keep the ghosts and demons at bay.

She was certain Fatima would seek her out, after dying such a brutal death. Even though Fatima was a secret friend, the spirit would likely haunt her until Molly changed her ways. Fatima had told Laurel about the Dover's power hoping to stop Molly from using it. Laurel wasn't as forgiving as Fatima believed and had tossed Molly out straight away.

The worn wood slats beneath her booted feet creaked and groaned under her slight weight. The rooms above the tavern may not be of the best quality. However, the modest space kept her safe and out of the elements. Magick kept her safe from everything else.

Later, Molly lay in bed waiting for sleep to overtake her. She should have taken the syrup to help her slumber. Her normal routine was hindered by Aaron's comments about her welfare. A sensation crept along her spine. Someone watched her.

She tossed on the narrow cot to stare out the window. The sands nearly covered the paneled glass and threatened to consume her only source of light.

A shadow moved across the pane blocking the moon from her view. Monsters took form in her memory. She shivered. She was unfamiliar with the creatures of this land, their strengths, and their weaknesses.

Molly sat up. There was a dark figure. She slid her feet into her worn leather boots. not bothering with the laces. Molly hugged herself in her shift against the cold. Why hadn't she stolen a morning robe from The Horizontal?

No one in the house would miss such luxury, or even care if she'd taken her entire wardrobe.

Molly was nearly upon the window when a creak sounded behind her.

She turned towards the sound. An evil figure entered her room, and the blessed door didn't completely shut, letting in a sliver of light, of hope. She pressed herself against the wall near the window, hoping to hide in the darkness. Her heartbeat was loud in her ears and she was certain he heard it.

"Hiding, are we? I don't much like games…"

Molly reached her left hand out searching for the small table which should have long ago been made into firewood. She shuffled to the left, but her foot caught in her laces and she tumbled to the side, hitting the sideboard.

The pitcher and bowl fell with a crash to the floor. The porcelain pieces reflected in the moonlight, like a map pointing toward her.

The man rose above her like a demon. She looked up.

Two blood-red eyes stared back at her through a sandstorm mask, and she was unable to discern their true color. What creature had red eyes? The man must be a kelpie, with such eyes.

She caught the glint of his sword.

Molly spun toward the fallen table and felt the blade slice along her right cheek and make a sweeping gash to her elbow. Ignoring her instinct to touch the wound, she fought through an agonizing tightness in her chest. Using all the power she possessed, she grasped the legs of the fallen table and smashed the base into her assailant's legs.

The creature landed on his back, and Molly willed him to stay down long enough for her to reach her athame, the only possession from her past.

She kicked off her unlaced boots and lunged towards the bed. The kelpie rose from his fall and tossed the table across the room. Molly flipped the cot on its side, using the thin mattress and rusted springs for protection. She reached for her knife. The handle peeked beneath the pillow.

"You have worn me out with your scheming ways," said the beast.

Molly grasped the athame and felt a strange comfort. She stood and thrust the knife at her attacker, but catching air instead, she cried out in frustration. Backing against the wall she took a breath and asked the dead to help guide her.

When she lifted her gaze she found those red eyes staring but not seeing her.

She aimed for his heart and screamed, "Faugh a Ballagh!"

The Cleaver turned at the last moment and her mark pierced the joint in his shoulder. His weapon arm hung limp. He reached for her neck with his right. His gloved fingers closed like a vice around her throat.

Molly tried to scream but was unable. She flung her arms towards him in anguish but did not reach him. Past events and bad choices assaulted her mind. She would die here and no one would care.

He lifted her off the floor, his meaty hand compressing her neck. She was almost out of air.

She heard shuffling on the stairs. Only a few more moments and she would be saved.

"What goes on Molly?" Tom London stood in the doorway. Assessing the situation, he raised a fist toward her assailant. "See now, put her down!" Tom ran towards her.

"Later my dear," the kelpie spoke before dropping her to the floor and crashing through the narrow window, likely sliding down the sand hill outside. Wind and dust blew into her room, by morning the sand would have buried the struggle between her and the demon. If only Molly was so fortunate.

"You are certainly lucky," Tom said. He pressed her blankets against her wounds.

She tried to speak, and nothing came out but a squeak. She settled for giving Tom a quizzical look.

"You, Molly Flannigan are the first to survive an encounter with the Cleaver and live to tell the tale."

"Are you certain? "

"Who else could it be?"

Molly silently blessed her elderly grandmother and promptly decided she would suffer her nightmares in silence if Laurel allowed her to return home.

* * *

CALLED TO LAUREL'S HOUSE, Benjamin Gunn decided he was cursed. He had left last night only to return this afternoon. He looked over his patient who had been brought to The Horizontal by a Jumbo. Laurel hovered like a mother-hen clucking at him each time Molly Flannigan winced or took a sharp intake of breath.

"Ben, be gentle with her," Laurel clucked, and in the next breath, "Are you okay Molly?"

"I'm fine." Molly was certainly the sort of girl Ben expected to see in this place. She was beautiful and held a fire that reminded him a bit of the fortune teller from Barnum's, with her one blue and one brown eye.

"You have heterochromia," he said to Molly. She likely knew. He wasn't sure why he mentioned it, maybe because he always found the condition unsettling.

"Chroma-what?"

"Dr. Gunn is referring to your different colored eyes." Laurel fluffed the pillows behind Molly's head. "It is one of the reasons Molly is popular with the men—her eyes, and other unusual gifts."

"All women in my family have different colored eyes." Molly shrugged as if the condition were normal.

"That is very unusual," he said, going back to tending her wounds, unable to look directly into her eyes. He feared she might see into the future like the old gypsy Rose at the circus. Once he completed his assessment, he left the room posthaste.

* * *

"YOU ARE MOVING BACK HERE," Laurel decreed once her husband clicked the door behind him. "I insist, of course, the Dover's powder has to go. Fatima is dead and this attempt on your life, it is too much." She couldn't afford to lose Molly.

"Laurel, I--" Molly's voice cracked. "I take the drug to sleep."

"Nonsense. There are other tonics and tisanes to help sleep come. Why I—"

"I can see the dead." Molly quickly blurted.

"I assure you that my husband is very much alive, although how is a mystery." Laurel sat on the bed, resting her hand on Molly's own.

"Laurel, I mean apparitions of the deceased."

The silence stretched.

"Are the spirits cruel to you?" Laurel was at heart spiritual. Her father was, after all, a missionary.

Laurel and Death were entwined. Death whispered her mother would die. When she told her father, he forced her to spend hours on her knees in prayer. In her youth, she did not understand. When her mother passed her father forbade her to cry, warning her of her true nature. Laurel learned to control that particular emotion, at least until recently, not only had her emotions betrayed her, but death had as well. He didn't warn of Fatima's death, as he had not warned of Ben's.

She looked intently at Molly. If Molly had informed Laurel of her gift, would the knowledge have made a difference? Laurel was sure this understanding would've swayed her decision but now it was too late.

"No. They can be quite a bit of a nuisance and I take the powder to shut out their voices, wails, and such," Molly explained.

"Perhaps they can protect you from the Cleaver," Laurel suggested.

"I'm sure he won't—"

"Molly, you are the one to escape. Criminals of these types rarely let go until they are stopped. Remember Jack..." Laurel's voice died away. She struggled to remind Molly of a killer who'd already taken the lives of girls in the same profession.

"Aye," Molly replied with her lips pursed.

Laurel shook her head. "I merely mean to point out that no one got away, and perhaps you are safer here. And of course, you have your spirits protecting you."

"Protecting me?"

"Did you not wonder if your gift is perhaps what helped you escape?" The more Laurel pondered it, the more she was satisfied Molly's gifts would keep her safe. Her own prediction of death had come in handy when reporting to the queen. Laurel had been able to sense death in soldiers who had come to her establishment and reported such to the queen along with any tactical plans the men revealed. "Now that this business is settled. I'll see you in the morning." Laurel rose to leave.

"No man is goin' to bed down with me face like this!" Molly pointed at the bandage, hiding the jagged scar running from her ear to her jawline.

"No man will need to. You are welcome to stay here, without working." Laurel sat again. She grasped Molly's hands and pressed her forehead to Molly's. "Although I suspect with your ghosts Molly, you didn't need to do much bedding for your work, did you?" How had Molly, who seemingly did little rotation through men, gathered a wealth of information? Until Molly revealed her cunning spiritual ability her intelligence gathering was almost unexplainable.

Molly possessed the good sense to stay quiet and Laurel took the opportunity to let Molly rest.

* * *

LAUREL WASN'T SURPRISED to see her husband outside the room she left. Not one bit. It was just like Ben to wait outside to see what had happened. He'd always been inquisitive. Now he had walked back into her life, perhaps feeling like her new family was his. Maybe it was his circus upbringing or maybe it was the fact he had no family here. Either way, she recalled he was always embracing the people around him like family. Ben settled her argument with her father regarding her purchase of Moody.

"What happened to Moody?" In all the excitement, she hadn't asked sooner.

"Moody is still in my employ."

"As what? Your valet?"

"Well, actually, yes, and he's also serving as my butler."

"Shame on you Ben! Making poor Moody perform such menial tasks."

"Hardly. It's not as if he has a lot to do. My apartments are right above my office."

"I meant to ask you--"

"Interrogate you mean," Ben mumbled under his breath, but she heard him.

"Fine, interrogate." There was no sense in arguing with him when he believed he was right. "Anyway, I meant to ask you, how long have you been in the city?"

"I wandered into the city, nearly seven years ago." Ben blushed a unique shade of red, almost burgundy.

"Seven years ago?! Christ Ben! Why didn't you come to me? You had to know I was in the city."

"I did know, but given our past--"

"The past where I thought you were dead?" She felt the first fractures in her calm facade which she projected to those around her.

"Exactly so. How could I come to you after leaving you at the Harem?" He seemed fascinated by the patterns in her carpet.

"Are you saying you knew my whereabouts this whole time?" A strong inclination rose inside her to see Ben's demise once again. She glared at him

"No, of course not. I learned you trained there. Once I realized your being in a harem was my fault, I couldn't come to you. I blame myself for not finding you sooner." His voice dropped.

"Ben, before you blame yourself and drag me along with you, perhaps you could tell me what has happened since you died." Laurel resolved to get the answers she desperately needed to complete the puzzle of her husband. She guided him along lavish hallways. Fine art hung on the walls complementing the variety of doors they passed. Doors in every color and shape. Here was where the true spy work took place.

"I'll order some tea." Remembering her American husband's distaste for tea, she added, "and Turkish coffee. I'm sure you're hungry after all the events of the evening. I will have Omar bring something to eat." Laurel couldn't suppress her satisfied smile. He seemed enamored with the colors around him; he didn't notice she had led him right to the door to her own personal quarters. She opened the dark mahogany door with a turquoise glass knob. "Please, join me."

* * *

BEN STARED AT HIS WIFE. Did he have the right to call her his? He wasn't sure. He looked at the room around him, her private sitting area. She sat across from him at a small round table, with two small curved chairs. There was a similar set, by the fireplace. The table was small enough for him to reach out and touch her fingers resting on the porcelain saucer. The air was thick with the scent of candles, perfume, and femininity. The evidence was plain. It was unusual for him to sit in this sacred room. She had led him into her lair. His clockwork heart made a small click, as the cogs skipped and quickly caught. Could she hear the sound?

"I have no memories before coming to the Great City. I understand from Moody that he found me on the border of the Russian and Ottoman Empire, in the Caucasus Mountains." He spoke loudly, hoping to cover any sounds his heart made.

"How did Moody find you?" Her eyes narrowed in on his cravat. She leaned in, resting her hand on his sleeve.

"He's never said. I'm not sure. When he found me, I was a shepherd."

"What?!" Laurel choked a bit on her tea and removed her hand from his arm. Damn it.

Ben started to rise, but she waved him off. "I'm fine. I'm trying to imagine you with sheep!"

"These aren't your timid English or even Scottish sheep. They are wild. Reminds me of the mountain sheep we have out West," he mused with a vivid recollection of how he missed the simple times.

"Have you been across the pond?" She asked.

"No, I've been here these past eight years." Why hadn't he sought out his family when his memory of them returned? Perhaps the lure of Laurel had grounded him in this spot.

"And you've known I was in the Global City for how long?"

Oh, there was no getting anything past Laurel. He couldn't stop her mind from turning, much like the gears and cogs turned for her in his heart.

She pondered the mystery before her. She asked questions and he made decisions. Laurel had served him well looking after patients in the field. He was sure her beauty and grace had something to do with her ease among them. She calmed a man with a smile and pried stories from them about their home and their family. She made them forget themselves with a simple touch.

"Only these past two years. I was too afraid to come to you, and I noticed…" He paused, looking down. He didn't want to shame her, and he wanted to keep his anger in check.

"Noticed…noticed what, Ben?"

"You took a lover." His voice came out a growl, and he kept his head bowed, trying to quench a desire for revenge.

"Ah…Aaron."

"Yes, Aaron." The man's name roared in his ears. Yet, though he disliked speaking about the man, he also enjoyed having the name of his adversary. Finally.

"How did you know about him?" her voice was a whisper.

Ben considered carefully his next words. He couldn't very well reveal the man reeked of her. The minute he'd caught her scent, he'd followed the aroma around the Embassy until he tracked the smell to the Russian Ambassador's office.

"I followed him from the Embassy. I'm not sure why. Perhaps he looked familiar. Perhaps it was a whim. I wasn't sure why I was compelled to track him to your very door. Upon your greeting, I knew what he was to you, my wife." The wretchedness of the day still haunted him.

"What were you doing at the Embassy?" Her question was clipped. He'd upset her, but Laurel was too refined to lash out at him. He wished she would. Her criticism would appease his self-loathing.

"I work as a physician there, for the American Envoy, George Bancroft. Moody found me and when my memories returned, I went to the American Envoy offices for sanctuary. I would've returned to the States, but there is nothing for me there. Since I first arrived, I believed you lost to me; there was no reason to search for you. I thought you were dead." He searched her face, hardly believing she sat near him. He looked for contempt in her chocolate brown eyes, derision on her lips, or disgust within her fine features and saw none. Ben had come home and could reveal his deepest secrets to her, his wife.

"It is a miracle we have found each other. I insist you stay here with me." Laurel reached out her hand and touched him. Calm spread over him and he stared where her finger folded between his own.

"Why?"

"I know it seems sudden, but honestly, I've missed you. I've missed time with you." Hurt appeared in her eyes.

An avalanche of over-protectiveness ruined his desire to stay with his wife. In his own stupidity, he'd forgotten the darkness within him that kept him in a remote area of town. He couldn't let the women in this house be exposed to his demons. He yanked his hand from her grasp, stood up, inhaled sharply, and backed away from her. His heart raced and his stomach clenched. He had already revealed too much to her.

"I have to go." He searched the aquamarine walls, finding the corner where she'd stashed his coat and hat. He hurried toward his belongings.

"Ben, what is wrong? Sit back down. I insist." She blocked his path.

"You are not in a position to insist on anything Madame." He was undeterred and moved past her with speed.

"I most certainly can. I am your wife!" Her voice rose above the swish of her skirts. She moved quickly to corner him.

He turned on her like a caged animal.

"Laurel, you may be my wife, but you belong to another. While I'm not happy about it, one thing is certain. I am no longer yours. My freedom comes before your wishes." He donned his coat with efficiency, before placing his bowler on his head.

"If my heart is in the way of your freedom, I shall not stop you." Her voice turned from warm honey to ice. Her entire demeanor changed. He had struck her deep, he was certain. She gestured towards the dark wooden door with her slender arm.

"Thank you." His moves were quick. When he finally put the door between them, a thump and slide downward echoed against the wood. Against his better judgment, he paused.

"I envy your freedom, husband. If I had mine, I would surely run you to ground, make you mine and bare my secrets to you." Her voice cracked through the keyhole and he fled, lest she changed her mind.

Ben shook his head. He should've fought the inspector coming here. Laurel would be safe if he hadn't arrived. He succeeded in breaking open old wounds and most assuredly his heart.

* * *

LAUREL SLUMPED AGAINST THE DOOR. What was wrong with her? She couldn't involve Ben in her life, she belonged to the queen now. Unless she could extradite herself from this life, she couldn't have Ben, no matter how much she wanted him. And she did want him, which had not changed in the years since their separation. She was drawn to him, like no other.

CHAPTER EIGHT

*R*aven waited nearly two hours for the good doctor to leave The Horizontal. Doctor Gunn marched at a ceaseless pace after leaving the brothel. When the doctor turned to look over his shoulder, Raven ducked into a shadowed alley. Raven pulled the collar of his duster over his neck. His Boss of the Plains Stetson rested low, shadowing his face. Doctor Gunn's scent was enough for him to follow, and Raven dropped back into the shadows.

Why was he taking such an indirect route? This pattern of tracking and hiding reminded Raven of chasing animals in the woods back home. It was as if Doctor Gunn knew he was being followed, which was impossible. Raven had been one of the best trackers in Company K, and before the war, his keen senses were well known within his tribe, despite his English blood.

Doctor Gunn's pace finally slowed in front of The Embassy of Nations, where all the world's political figures convened.

Seward and former President Lincoln had sent him to find where their allies would lie should the United States side with the Inuit and settlers in Archangel. Lincoln wanted to use the land to settle former slaves, as well as others displaced by the war.

As the head of the Freedmen's Bureau, Lincoln was very passionate about helping everyone transition under Reconstruction. Lincoln would be able to continue his work with the Freedmen's Bureau, which President Johnson liked just fine. The assassination attempt on Lincoln kept him away from politics. John Wilkes Booth, a low-down sneak, attempted to shoot Lincoln, nearly killing the man. Lincoln had stood to protect his wife and the shot hit him in the chest, missing his heart, but nicked his spine. Lincoln resigned from the Presidency. Since his confinement to a wheelchair, the former president had taken on the cause of all veterans regardless of whether they were Union or Confederate.

Archangel was believed to be rich in gold, as well as copper and zinc, and the territory was viewed as a new resource to be settled. Raven knew and he suspected Laurel did as well, that it would be a haven for the Fae as the royals had no connection to the United States giving Fae the freedom they had earned helping the Americans fight their wars.

Raven continued sleuthing along the cobbles, as Doctor Ben continued past the Embassy. Had Seward and Lincoln sent him on a fool's errand? His instincts told him this was about more than finding out where sympathies might lie. To take on the Great Alliance was to take on most of Europe and Asia and disrupt the balance of power those nations held dear.

Raven refused to let go of the Archangel cause. Once Archangel was secure, there would be land for President Johnson who was trying to unify the country and a home for all fae creatures outside the reach of the royals.

Raven was about to give up tracking Doctor Gunn to his home when he felt heat tingle along his spine.

"Why do you follow Doctor Gunn?" an accented voice asked. The tone was as cold as the blade at his throat.

"Now let us not be hasty, mister. I admit to being a mite forgetful when a knife is being held close to my neck," Raven rasped. He hoped the man would understand and let down his guard. His tactic worked. The weapon was lowered.

Raven lifted his shoulders, turning left and pushing the leather of his duster into the blade. He felt pressure against his skin. Yet, the leather held. He lowered his face into his shoulder and pushed against his attacker. He reached into his own boot and pulled out his Bowie. He pivoted on his boot heel and put some distance between them to find Ben's assistant staring hard at him.

"Moody isn't it, I seem to recall your name from Doctor Gunn's," Raven said.

Moody's dark eyes seemed to glow with fire. He held a curved blade towards Raven.

"Are you his property?" Raven smelled sulfur emanating off Moody's skin. He knew that fae were traded like commodities among those more powerful. He lowered his knife a bit.

"No. Lady Gunn purchased me as a child and I grew in her care. The Gunn's are my family."

Once Raven heard the word purchase he didn't hear the word 'family' and was disheartened by Moody's lack of independence. He hadn't known Laurel held slaves. The knowledge definitely colored his opinion of her. Did he want an alliance with a slaveholder or a fae so powerful as to keep others? He spat on the ground.

"I ask again, why are you following Doctor Gunn?" Moody's voice was quiet. His gaze and weapon were unwavering.

Was the man purposely deceiving him? "I plan no harm to your master." Raven sheathed his Bowie. "What do you say to proper introductions?" Raven extended his hand.

"I am Moody Jinn." Moody finally sheathed his own curved blade on the top of a sheath at his waist. "What are you doing here, Inspector Raven Clarke?"

Raven was bowled over by the question and pulled back his hand before Moody could touch him. He found Moody's presence unsettling, though there was no longer a weapon aimed at his person. "How do you know my name?"

"I know your name because you know it." Moody's voice was matter of fact.

"What are you?" Raven searched his own mind for the stories of his own people. He struggled with the possibility that this creature before him was powerful enough to read thoughts. . The hairs on the back of his neck stood on end. He looked behind him for an escape.

"I will tell you what I am if you tell me what you are. Shall we go see Doctor Gunn together?" Moody extended his hand towards the cobble path.

"No, I believe I've seen enough." Raven's superstitions and agitation led him to retreat back to the brothel.

* * *

THE CLEAVER SULKED in a corner of the abandoned castle waiting for his master to appear. He detested the wait. He was a man of action. He paced the floor, his boots clicking across the stones and echoing off the high walls. Where was his Master?

"You are impatient." His master called from the hall steps.

"Yes." The Cleaver didn't dare deny it. He knew what would happen if he stepped out of line.

"I understand you attempted to kill your last target." Master raised his voice. He walked into the moonlight. Was he angry? Emotions were hard to decipher with Master. He was a tiny man. With a raspy voice and his face was always covered, his features elusive. He wore a fedora, low over his eyes, making him difficult to identify.

"It was unavoidable," he replied.

"Lies!" Master raised his hand and held the one thing able to bring the Cleaver to his knees.

"No... Please." The Cleaver begged. How he hated the thing which made him weak.

Master ignored his cries and blew the whistle.

The Cleaver's knees buckled. He gripped the side of his skull wanting to tear it open. How long? How long would Master punish him for his indiscretions?

"Kill the queen's courtesan! Those are your orders. Why are you dallying with the whores? Molly Flannigan will be a fine soldier in my army. I can use her, mold her into my will. If you kill her, you will feel my wrath!" Master's shrill yelling was nearly as bad as the whistle. The Cleaver remained on his knees, not daring to move.

"Look at me." Master placed his gloved hands beneath the Cleaver's chin.

The Cleaver lifted his head at the touch.

"Imagine if a girl like Molly could be yours. Would you not like a mate, you wretched creature?" Master's voice was soft, barely audible above the ringing in Cleaver's ears.

The Cleaver nodded, trying to pull away.

"Do not!" Master gripped Cleaver's jaw, before releasing him. "If not for me, you would be dead."

The Cleaver stilled.

"Stand."

The Cleaver obeyed.

"I understand I may have some mending to do on your shoulder." Master nodded towards the shoulder where Molly had stabbed him.

"No. I took care of it." He rotated his shoulder to demonstrate his recovery.

"Aren't you a wealth of resources? You know, you were the greatest accomplishment at the Osiris Hospital. I will hold a fondness in my heart for you - my first successful resurrection. They said the surgery couldn't be done, especially by me. As if I was inferior to all those other doctors." Master whispered, tucking an errant red hair away from Cleaver's face.

Cleaver was disturbed by his master's actions. This wasn't the first time the man touched him affectionately. As if Master wanted more than the Cleaver would give him.

"I'll not disappoint you again Master."

"See that you don't. You have served me well so far. I would hate to see your service come to an end. I've grown terribly fond of you." Master turned and walked away.

Once Master was gone, the Cleaver released a breath he had not realized he held.

CHAPTER NINE

*L*aurel lounged on her favorite fainting sofa in the parlor used for entertaining her guests. The last of the patrons filtered out of her establishment. Long hours had passed since Ben left, and with each chime of the clock, she fell deeper into her cups.

"Miss Laurel." Omar paused in front of her.

"More Cognac, please, Omar," She lifted her glass in a very unladylike fashion.

"Go upstairs, Miss."

"I should be mad at you. If you had left me with Ben, we would still be together," she slurred.

"Yes, Miss."

"No argument from you?" She stood, or rather teetered, in front of him.

"No, Miss."

"I hate you," she mumbled and collapsed back onto her settee.

"I understand, Miss."

Laurel tried to rise when she heard the door open. "Ben?"

Inspector Raven Clarke entered the parlor from the foyer.

"What are you doing here Inspector?" Her words trickled from her lips, much like the Cognac from her glass when she swayed.

"Is she foxed?" Raven asked Omar.

"Yes, sir."

"I'm not foxed, I'm British. Inspector, I simply must inquire, are all Americans as stubborn as my beloved husband?" Laurel asked.

"I have no idea what you are talking about Lady Gunn." Raven's answer was stiff.

Omar stood and straightened his shoulders and walked towards the door. He should be unflinchingly scary, but at the moment, Laurel had nothing to fear.

"I say, Omar, where are you going?" Everyone seemed to leave her.

"To bed miss," Omar answered, continuing his retreat.

"Don't get snippy with me," she shouted after him. "Have a seat, Inspector." Laurel threw her right arm wide towards the rosewood balloon-back chair with the maroon button-tufted seat.

"Why are you intoxicated?" Raven asked.

"Why are you here?" She narrowed her eyes at him, irked by his cool and aloof manner.

"If you will recall, I'm staying here," Raven replied.

"Ah yes. Please continue onward then." Laurel pointed towards the lower-level rooms which she occasionally leased to guests.

"Do you need assistance to get to your room, madam?"

"Certainly not from a rogue, like you." If not for Ben's sudden appearance she might be tempted. Inspector Raven Clarke was a fine specimen.

"Well then, I shall be on my way." He turned to leave.

"Stop!"

He halted and turned back to her.

"Will you refill my glass?" She lifted her glass towards him, tilting the tumbler in her hand, showing emptiness.

"No, Lady Gunn, I won't. You can walk a few feet to the bar." Raven spoke in a rather condescending tone.

"Actually, I can't. I'm afraid I will fall flat on my face," she said in a hushed voice. She lowered her head, along with her glass, and stared at her lap.

"Let me help you to your rooms," he said solemnly.

"Perhaps that would be best." Laurel's chest was numb. She might be ready to give up the evening, but she had no intention of giving up Ben.

Once in her room, she knew the truth. This was all Ben's fault. He was like a pebble in her boot. Laurel needed to dig before getting him out. No, she didn't want him out, she wanted him in. In her bed. In her life. In her heart.

She needed to keep him close, keep an eye on him and keep him safe. She smiled half-heartedly. Her husband was a fae. When they first met she wasn't as sure about her gift, but now she knew. Laurel never saw his death, it should have been a clue. But what was he? She must spy on her own husband to see what's what. The man wouldn't stand a chance in the battle against her feminine arsenal. Tomorrow was a new day and she planned to renew her assault on her husband. A good night's sleep and she would feel refreshed.

* * *

LAUREL AWOKE the next day with a pounding in her head. What had she been thinking, getting "foxed" as the American, Raven, had put it? She rang the cord by her bed and proceeded to try and stand. Her cook, Libby, appeared before she accomplished the task.

"What are you doing here?" Laurel asked. "Where's Sophia?" Sophia Ostwald was the Prussian girl she had hired to serve as a maid. She was training with Libby while learning to master the duties. Sophia was a bit snobbish for a maid. She was lovely though, with hair black as night and gray eyes. However, given her distaste for cleaning the beds and socializing with other girls, Laurel dared not suggest the role of a courtesan.

"Sophia quit. Probably for the best, Mum. That one was a bit uppity for servants' duties."

Laurel didn't disagree. Given the fact that Fatima was dead and Molly barely escaped the Cleaver, perhaps it was best Sophia was not here, especially given she was human with an odd death before her - Air. Either by strangulation or disease. Besides, fewer girls were easier to protect. Laurel decided to visit Molly and see how she fared. However, she needed to rise from the bed before she did anything else. Which was proving more of a challenge than she anticipated this morning.

"I gave you some strong tea there, Mum." Libby pointed at the pot.

"Bless you, Libby."

"Also, some bread. It should settle your stomach if the organ is bothering you." Libby placed a large silver tray on the side table. "It is nice having Miss Molly back."

Laurel silently agreed. She missed Molly more than anyone, and she now understood the reason for Dover's powder. Laurel was happy to have her friend back. With Fatima gone, she'd missed afternoon tea with her friends.

"Are you feeling well for dinner at Envoy Kage's house?" Libby asked.

Laurel groaned, causing her head to throb. Sitting through a boring state dinner sounded horrible. However, political events were part of her role to gather information on the enemy. She had known Kage's mother in the harem. He was like a younger brother to her. Now Kage was Emissary to the city of Constantinople. He reported directly to the Sultan.

In her first years of running The Horizontal, Kage came and had been one of the regular clients. She never charged him, because he would simply return to his uncle's harem. Kage's patronage ensured both Europeans and Turks visited her establishment. Kage engaged with all the ladies of her house until Miss Victoria Thorpe came along.

"Mum? Should I send your regrets?" Libby stood looking at her.

"No Libby, I will attend the dinner. It will be good to see Victoria, a spot of sun in all this sadness." Laurel remembered when Kage fell hard for Victoria. He paid to have Victoria available exclusively to him. Laurel was astonished when Victoria also fell for the French Turk. By all accounts, Kage and Victoria fell in love and were happily married. Laurel longed to see her friend but did not look forward to seeing the amorous couple when all her wounds were still raw and on the surface. She went over yesterday's events in her head and still could not fathom why her husband abandoned her.

"First I must face the day," Laurel said. She planted her feet on the carpet and walked toward the side table where Libby placed the tray.

"Do you want me to send one of the other girls to help you dress in Sophia's place?" Libby asked.

"No, I can manage on my own. I managed between when Victoria left and Sophia started. I will be fine." Laurel lifted the pot and poured tea into the delicate china cup. "Libby?"

Libby paused at the door, "Yes, Mum?"

"Would you check on Molly and let her know I will visit this morning?" Laurel asked.

"Yes, Mum," Libby said before closing the door behind her.

* * *

MOLLY WAS awake and sitting up in bed when Laurel entered the blue room. "I wish you hadn't put me in here."

"Why ever not?" Laurel looked around the room confused.

59

"This room was Victoria's. Don't feel right, me being here." Molly winced as her "bad breeding" showed in her language. Whenever she was uncomfortable, she slipped back into the voice from the streets. The young girl she'd once been survived. Molly wasn't sure some days she would.

"Well, not anymore, it's not. This is presently a guest room. I debated putting Inspector Raven in the blue room but decided he did not require comfort for his job. Besides he could stay in the Embassy officer quarters if need be."

"Is that where he's staying then? At the Embassy?" Molly asked.

"No. I don't trust him. I want him to be visible. He's in the barracks with Omar." Laurel's mouth turned up at the corners.

"That must be interesting." Molly couldn't resist the smile. She was flabbergasted. Laurel would consider letting a man stay within the walls of The Horizontal without paying for the privilege. If men stayed with the girls, there was a cost for that. "I thought we didn't have guests within the walls?"

"Queen Victoria has been after me to allow members of Parliament to stay here when they visit The Global City. I'm allowed to use it at my discretion when it is unoccupied."

"So, it will still be Victoria's room." Molly stifled a giggle.

"Yes. Perhaps I should rename the room." Laurel giggled a bit too.

It was good to laugh again and Molly was glad she had come home.

Molly had once broken Laurel's hard exterior shell. Crumbling Laurel's walls wasn't hard, they'd been wonderful friends and Molly had been her confidant at one time. Yet, now Laurel remained inside the door, never venturing further into the room.

"Speaking of Victoria, I have been invited to Envoy Kage's for dinner. Would you like to join us, if the trip isn't too taxing for you?"

"In all honesty, Laurel, I'd rather spend the day moving back to my old room than getting ready for a stuffy embassy party." Better she was surrounded by wards than to suffer another restless night. She was convinced the dead were coming back simply to torture her. What had she ever done to them?

"I don't blame you at all. I wish I could avoid the pomp of it," Laurel said.

Molly simply smiled.

"Perhaps I shall invite Victoria to tea, tomorrow?"

"Now, that I would enjoy," Molly spoke in all sincerity.

"I'll send Omar to you once he has cleared your old rooms," Laurel spoke before closing the door behind her.

Molly spent the day alongside Omar. Apparently, Laurel kept all her belongings, clothes, and personal effects. Her possessions gave Molly hope. Perhaps her friend had not given up on her, like many others.

Ironically her room was vacated a few days before by a maid who left abruptly. All the girls' rooms were located above a courtyard, with the rooms below referred to as the barracks. There was only one way to access the courtyard rooms above, through the main house. Of course, when men spent the night in the barracks, the girls still flaunted "the goods" so to speak, and the men cat-called from below. Molly met Aaron during her second week here, calling out to him below.

Aaron was a handsome man, despite not having the use of both arms. She had teased him when they met saying he must have Irish blood in him with his fire-red hair. He had assured her he was English, or rather half of him was. His mother was a Russian lady of the court and his father's mistress. Aaron told her not all born on the wrong side of the blanket were as lucky as he. While he couldn't inherit, for his father had legitimate sons, he was afforded proper schooling and a commission was purchased on his behalf.

Molly had set a chair outside her room to take her dinner on the veranda. Across the courtyard on the upper tier, she watched as Laurel made the rounds, knocking on girls' rooms, seeing who would be working, and how they fared.

Laurel was unlike any madam she'd ever met and this house was unlike any she'd seen before. Molly had worked on the streets in London briefly before meeting with the Brotherhood of the Veil. She had worked at a theater for the Brotherhood and even Ruddy MacLauchlan, who was a mean bastard. He took all the money, claiming the funds were for the Brotherhood, and the actors had no freedom. They were expected to fraternize with the British and give the information to Ruddy, along with all their additional earnings. The conditions were abysmal. When Ruddy first approached Molly about coming to work at The Horizontal, she was happy to escape his clutches.

Queen Victoria likely believed her spies in skirts were a secret, but since all her nobles and men of government blathered at the first sign of feminine flesh. The secret was definitely in doubt. . When the Brotherhood found out about the house of female spies they recruited Molly. She would have to report back to them soon. Months had gone by since her last missive. Was The Cleaver a hired assassin from her radical employers? Molly didn't have time to dwell on it, as Laurel approached her with another courtesan in tow.

"Molly, are you all settled in?" Laurel asked as she approached. Molly was so caught up in her own thoughts she'd completely missed her approach.

"Yes, quite. I see you two are all dressed up?" Molly nodded to the girl standing behind Laurel.

"Oh, yes." Laurel turned toward the dark-skinned girl. "This is Dominique Augustine, and she will be escorting Inspector Raven Clarke to the Embassy this evening."

Molly remembered seeing Raven Clarke exiting his room, in the courtyard below, a mysterious-looking fellow, and terribly dashing with his eye patch. "Will this be your first time at The Embassy of the Holy Alliance of Nations?"

"Yes, ma'am it will be," Dominique answered with an American southern lilt. The girl was quite striking with her dark skin and gray eyes. Her ebony hair was pulled back in a sharp chignon.

"Shall I give Aaron your regards and let him know you have returned?" Laurel asked.

"I'm sure we'll see each other soon enough." Molly did not want Aaron to see the fresh scars. She wasn't sure if she could shoulder his pity.

"Alright, supper should be around soon. Libby's been a bit short-handed since Sophia quit." Laurel patted Molly's shoulder before taking her leave. Laurel and Dominique rounded the veranda and headed back into The Horizontal.

A chill wafted against Molly's back. She turned to look over her shoulder. "Fatima, I wondered if you were going to show. Shall we have a chat?"

* * *

LAUREL SAT IN THE CARRIAGE, gazing out across the cobblestone streets. The vehicle moved gracefully along the cobbles from The Horizontal to the Embassy. The Arabian horses' hooves clicked like a metronome.

Lamplighters were starting to light the dark corridors and alleyways, clearing the path of shadows and creating flickers in dark corners.

Lemon boards glowed with golden scrawled letters. These were giant paper rolls illuminated from behind by lanterns. The lemon juice writing would appear as the lanterns heated the paper. Men or beasts of burden would continually turn the paper. Laurel turned from the familiar scenery to converse with the couple across from her.

"You seem satisfied with yourself, Inspector, much like the cat who caught the canary," she said.

"Very much so, I'm happy to travel by carriage. I find those Jumbos most unsettling. Give me a horse any day."

"Did you know the Jumbos were invented by an American?" she asked.

"Why?" He shuddered as he voiced his question.

"They were invented by Professor Edmund Phelan. He lives in the Russian American settlement. I believe you call it New Archangel."

The couple stiffened.

"Well, the professor had a daughter, Abigail. She was fascinated with exotic animals, and when she and her father lived in India, she wanted an elephant of her own. Professor Phelan built a small brass pachyderm, named Trumbo, for his daughter to ride around on. He eventually built larger models and they became popular as a mode of transportation. Once the queen purchased an African Elephant from Barnum for the London Zoo, the name Jumbo sort of took hold. Believe it or not, there are more Jumbos in the settlement of Alchemia than in Constantinople."

"Thank you for warning me," Raven commented.

"Warning you? Are you headed to Alchemia?" Laurel asked.

"That is my next scheduled assignment," he replied.

"And what about you Dominique? Do you have another assignment?" Laurel started to wonder exactly what these two were playing at, besides spying on the Russians and finding allies to their cause.

"I'm assigned to Inspector Raven for the duration of his tours," Dominique replied. She looked at her folded hands on her lap.

"Assigned to him as what?" Laurel asked.

"She's my personal assistant," Raven replied before Dominique could respond.

"Oh, is that what you two are calling this?" Laurel pointed her finger, gesturing between the two of them.

The conversation abruptly halted along with the carriage. Laurel glanced out the window to see they had arrived at Kage's personal home within the Embassy walls.

"This conversation is not over," Laurel said. The carriage rolled to a stop and the door swung open to a waiting footman.

* * *

WHY HAD he come to this ridiculous party? Ben barely knew Envoy Kage Francis Kearns, but Moody recommended he attend. He managed to stand in the corner and avoid scrutiny. His friend, now a French diplomat Comte Pierre Jean Claude spoke with English Commodore Emery Pembrooke and the Englishman's female companion.

Ben's head spun with the pressure of saying the right things to the right people. Even worse, saying the absolute wrong thing at the wrong time. The evening ahead reminded him of school back in Edinburgh and making small talk at socials about the weather, food, or heaven forbid fashion. Moments like this made him miss the circus and the family-type atmosphere. No one at the big top ever wanted to make small talk. Everyone was familiar with everyone else. Conversations held topics of substance. He scanned the room. Inspector Raven Clarke was introduced, along with a woman of mixed race, Dominique Augustine.

Ben straightened upon seeing the inspector; the man tended to put him on his toes. Would wonders never cease? Ben was mildly prepared when Lady Laurel Gunn was announced. She didn't appear immediately though. Ben strained his neck to try and get a look. She hadn't followed.

Only after the host and hostess were announced for dinner, did Laurel come in, her hand resting on Ms. Victoria Kearns's arm. Kage Kearns walked in behind the ladies shaking his head over their lack of protocol, yet forgiving in the smile he seemed to suppress. Laurel obviously loved these people. Ben could tell by the way she leaned forward when they spoke, the subtle touches she gave each, and the bestowed smiles. To say he was envious was an understatement. He was sure his skin was tinged green.

Laurel stopped in conversation and looked to where Emory Pembrooke and the Count stood. She paused and seemed to stiffen. Ben watched his wife smooth her hands on her skirt. She was upset. He set out towards her, protocol be damned.

Ben paused in mid-rescue at the sound of Lieutenant Aaron March's voice from behind him. "Lovey."

Of course, he would've come. He was after all Laurel's lover and business partner. Ben slowly stepped backward, as the Lieutenant marched by. He watched the play-by-play from the middle of the room.

"Aaron," Laurel turned away from Pembrooke and the Count.

"Sorry, I'm late, my dear. Busy at work, and all that." Aaron leaned in, placed a hand on Laurel's arm and gave her a peck on the cheek.

Ben clenched his fists at his side. His knuckles itched to go and punch Lieutenant-kiss-a-lot.

"I understand," Laurel said, leaning back to look at Lieutenant March.

Ben released his fisted hands and inhaled. His wife never understood anything, not with that tone. No, his wife was a first-class interrogator. 'Busy with what? What kind of work? How many surgeries have you performed? Have you ever seen a corpse? Have you ever dipped your toes in the Nile? When you were in the circus, was there a bearded lady?'

In Ben's brief history, his wife was a fountain of questions. No 'I understand' from her. Ben moved further into the corner and watched the couple interact, looking for cracks in their relationship. All foundations had them.

"Victoria was telling me she thinks they may be expecting." Laurel moved her arm from Aaron's grasp to Victoria's.

"I say, Kage, old man, well done." Aaron took his abandoned limb and turned to shake Kage's hand.

"We don't know anything yet, Tori is merely hopeful." Envoy Kage raised a quizzical brow to Aaron's outstretched hand.

Lieutenant March, undaunted, merely placed his hand at his side, and leaned into Laurel. "I say, I shall go talk to Pembrooke then."

"Fine." Laurel smiled at the lieutenant, granting him leave.

Ben coughed, covering his laugh at Aaron's dismissal.

Laurel raised her gaze to where he stood. Ben could see the questions forming behind those glittering green eyes. He might as well go over and make his acquaintance with her friends.

* * *

WHAT WAS HE DOING HERE? Who invited him? How did he know Kage? Why did he have to tempt her? Those questions and a million more, formed in Laurel's mind. Her breath caught. She watched Ben devour the distance between them in long strides. She took a deep breath.

Laurel nodded in greeting to her husband. She reached out and closed his outstretched hand within her own as he approached, to prevent him from inappropriate behavior.

"Ben, good to see you. I didn't expect to see you here. Did you get a special invite or are you representing someone else?" She asked.

"I was invited." The corner of his mouth turned up.

"By whom?" Who could Ben possibly know in her small intimate group?

"That would be me, Madame." Count Jeanne Pierre Claude joined their little circle.

"Oh? How do you know my husband?" Laurel asked.

Victoria gasped.

Kage choked.

And somewhere behind her, a glass dropped to the floor.

Laurel realized her blunder nearly immediately.

"I'm sorry Madame Gunn. I did not realize you were married and certainly not to my brother."

"Your brother?" Now was Laurel's turn to gasp for air and choke.

"Brother in Arms. We were stationed in India together. Then this rapscallion met a pretty girl and went and married... Mon Dieu! Ben, is this she...the mademoiselle from India?"

"Yes." Her husband spoke quietly.

"I cannot believe she is here. After all this time. How lucky for both of you!" Count Pierre Jean smiled wide, before clapping Ben on the back. Laurel couldn't help but smile at the man's enthusiasm. Her husband looked decidedly uncomfortable.

"Lucky indeed. I'm not sure my husband shares your passion for our rekindled romance." If Ben refused to come to her, she would garner support where she could. What better allies than his brother. Laurel raised her glass of sherry to her lips, hiding her quiet smirk.

"Say it isn't so, mon ami. You are a man of fiery passion, this I remember from our time in Algeria. There was a camp follower, Marie, I believe her name was, and she was fascinated by our dear Doctor Gunn. She could not resist his vitality. I had finished reporting to the Caporal Chef when I returned to our tent, and my brother Ben was engaged in--"

"I'm sure my wi- Lady Gunn, has a very good idea of what I was engaged in." Ben cut off the Count, "After all she watches patrons engage in it every day. Don't you, my dear?"

Laurel cocked her head to peer at her husband. There was heat in his eyes, and he clearly was trying to provoke a response.

"I don't usually watch my clients engaged, so to speak. However, it has been a significant amount of time since we've engaged. Perhaps I could use a refresher," Laurel stated boldly. She'd wager her husband hadn't expected such a response.

"Mon ami, how can you resist such temptation?" Count Pierre Jean asked.

"It takes tremendous willpower. I assure you. I have the strength to resist the woman who refuses me as I refuse to share her," Ben responded.

Oh-ho! Jealousy was the thorn in his paw. So her husband wanted her all to himself. A warm glow surged deep inside her. She moved cautiously towards Ben. Laurel dare not spook him when she was close to getting what she desired. When she reached him, she blocked his path and leaned in close, sealing off his retreat., "Come home with me, and I'll not let another man into my bed," she whispered.

CHAPTER TEN

"Perhaps we should be seated for dinner." Kage broke the unanswered question hanging between Laurel and Ben. His wife retreated to find her seat.

Ben didn't expect her to withdraw, but he fully intended to pursue her. Laurel took her seat to the left of Kage, who sat at the head of the table. Envoy Kearns' wife sat next to him on his right. Before Aaron could take the seat next to Laurel, Ben swooped in and took it. Unfortunately, he would have to sit next to Lieutenant Aaron March, which was fine.

Did Laurel mean what she said? His desire stirred at the thought of having her once again and the wicked things he would do to her.

Inspector Raven Clarke sat directly across from Ben.

Lieutenant March didn't seem put off by Ben's subterfuge; he simply took the chair to the right of Ben, without as much as a word.

"As if," Ben huffed.

"What dear?" Laurel asked.

"Nothing, merely thinking to myself," Ben mumbled.

"I hope your thoughts were terribly scandalous." Laurel pressed her hand on top of his thigh.

"I'll have to let you know." He coughed. Despite their time apart, she still read him like a book.

"Victoria, I should let you know Ben is one of the finest doctors to come out of Edinburgh," Laurel spoke across the table to her friend. "Victoria is expecting," Laurel said, speaking to Ben.

"We hope," Envoy Kearns corrected.

"They hope," Laurel concurred.

"Well if your wife is with child, I'd be happy to assist if you do not have a physician currently," Ben said.

A feminine laugh disrupted his thought and Ben looked over to where his friend Pierre Jean was flirting shamelessly with the dark-skinned woman on Raven's left.

"Dominique, you must let me call on you. You are far too beautiful to waste your talents on gamblers, wastrels, and..." Pierre Jean shuddered, "politicians."

"Are you not a politician sir?" Dominique asked.

"Oui, but I'm also a lover," Pierre Jean quipped flirtatiously. Pierre Jean's gaze moved down the woman's curvy form, and Ben imagined his friend was quite smitten.

"So are my clients," she said.

"And yet, I am a lover of all things beautiful, such as you Mademoiselle Augustine," Pierre Jean leaned in and whispered. He raised Dominique's hand to his lips.

Ben shook his head at Pierre Jean's antics.

"What?" Raven asked from across the table.

"My friend is flirting with your companion." Ben chuckled.

Raven looked to his left at Dominique. "So, he is."

"Aren't you worried?" Ben asked.

"No Miss Augustine is a free agen—woman. I have no hold on her," Raven replied.

"I see my mistake. I assumed since you both arrived together and were both American..."

"Miss Augustine is free to see whom she wishes." Raven's voice sounded resigned to Ben's ears.

"Just so, I believe Pierre Jean is intent on making her his mistress," Ben informed him.

"Do not give away all my secrets Gunn," Pierre Jean called over. He held Dominique's hand, caressing her arm.

"Husband, why are you torturing your friend?" Laurel asked. She ventured her hand further north.

"I'm not. However, I think the Inspector should know when his lady friend is about to dally with a passionate Frenchman," Ben said. He halted her movements by placing his hand on hers.

Jean Pierre looked at Ben and raised his glass. "Just so."

Laurel laughed on Ben's left. He turned back to her.

"Did you mean what you said about my being your only lover?" Ben asked. He simply had to know. The thought of spending every night with her would be more than pleasurable. She had a way of chasing away his nightmares.

"You think I'm lying?" Laurel asked.

"No, I simply wonder why me? You could have any man here." He leaned in and breathed against her ear.

"Don't you understand, husband?" She pulled back. The hurt was evident in her liquid brown eyes.

"I believe I do, but I want to be clear." Ben didn't know why he risked her safety to satisfy his own heart. He seemed helpless around this woman. Ben wanted to believe he wouldn't hurt her. Those damnable blackouts made him uncertain.

Laurel drew closer to him, her lips were close, brushing his ear as she cooed, "Ben, you must know, I still love you." Without warning, she kissed him. In front of the table at large and her current lover, she kissed him.

Her kiss was a simple touch of the lips, but to him, the gesture conveyed much more. A pink stain spread over her cheeks. Was she embarrassed or did she feel the same longing in her soul?

A cough sounded to his right. He looked over at Lieutenant Aaron March. The man likely wanted a duel at dawn. In Ben's opinion, Laurel's words and display were worth an injury or perhaps death.

"Are congratulations in order?" Aaron leaned forward to look past Ben and focused his gaze solely on Laurel.

"We'll see," Laurel responded. She flattened her hands on her lap, smoothing imaginary wrinkles out of the pristine white napkin.

* * *

THE REMAINDER of dinner was uneventful, and following the meal, they retired to the salon for coffee. The women gathered around a table, with coffee service. The men were enjoying brandy on the other side of the room. Dominique sat next to Laurel and Victoria across from them.

Ben had been quiet the remainder of the meal, and stoic. Was he unaffected by her declaration?

"It is good to see you, Laurel." Sophia Ostwald said in greeting, before seating herself next to Victoria.

"You as well, Sophia. I'm surprised to find you on the arm of Pembrooke?" Laurel narrowed her eyes on Sophia and took a sip of her bitter coffee. The beverage lacked something sweet, much like the dark-haired Prussian woman, now seated next to Victoria.

"Yes. Well, I had applied for a maid position at his townhouse, something a bit more respectable, you understand. He thought I would suit him better in other ways." Sophia took the cup Victoria offered her.

"It seems a far step up, considering you'd never approached me with an interest in training at The Horizontal. I was told by others you looked down on my profession." Laurel didn't bother to hide the disdain in her voice.

"You seemed to have found fresh talent." Sophia nodded to Dominique beside Laurel. The Prussian girl didn't even bother to deny the rumors. In Laurel's mind, this confirmed Sophia was either very naive or very smart. Laurel remained undecided.

"I am very talented," Dominique said before taking a chocolate truffle from a plate on the table and popping the dark treat into her mouth.

"Lady Laurel only hires the best," Sophia said graciously.

Laurel noted she seemed to fit the role of a lady. Sophia had raw talent, much like Victoria before her. Perhaps Laurel should put her pettiness aside and leave the Prussian woman alone. It was unlikely Laurel would not have elevated her to the role of courtesan within her house, given Sophia's human status.

"That I do. Dominique has proven very popular," Laurel spoke with cool authority.

"I can only imagine," Sophia said before raising the cup to her lips. After a rather loud sip which caused Laurel to cringe, the Prussian set the cup back on the saucer with such force that the china clinked. Raw talent, indeed.

"I couldn't stay there after Fatima's death," Sophia spoke, either uncaring or unaware of her words.

Victoria sat rigidly in her chair.

Laurel, much attuned to her friend's senses, winced.

"Excuse me." Victoria rose and rushed from the room.

Kage excused himself from the group of men and raced after his wife.

Leaving guests unattended was bad form, but Laurel completely understood.

The men filed into military formation. Their march caused a giggle to erupt from Dominique and a smile from Laurel. They observed the former soldiers' approach.

"It seems as if we've been abandoned." Aaron sat across from Laurel, in Victoria's chair.

Laurel frowned. What was Aaron up to?

"What shall we do now?" he looked to Sophia as he asked.

"Perhaps a game is in order, to occupy us until our hosts return," Dominique spoke up.

Raven leaned on the arm of the settee. His long legs stretched out in front of him, blocking any others from sitting down. "We hear you English are quite fond of them."

"We are," Aaron said with a smile still looking at Sophia.

"Perhaps a game of Look-a-bout would be in order." Laurel rose to her feet.

"Never heard of it." Sophia sat motionlessly, yet her eyes darted about the room.

"Typically, the host shows everyone a small object in the room. All the guests are to leave, while it is hidden. When everyone returns, they look for the item until they spot it. Then, they sit down. The last one to sit loses, and therefore hides another small object and so the game continues," Laurel explained.

"So, like Hide-and-Seek, but with an object," Dominique said.

"Very similar," Ben replied.

Laurel knew he remembered how they played the game following dinner before their wedding. Instead of playing, they drifted away to the garden, leaving her father furious and embarrassed. The kisses they shared were absolutely worth the lecture Laurel received later.

"There are not enough chairs to play here. We will have to go to the dining room," Aaron said.

"Why not divide into teams?" Raven asked.

"Why not do both? Let's even expand to the lower levels of the house. Move an object from one room to another?" Aaron had risen to stand by Sophia.

"Now see here," Commodore Pembrooke spoke from outside the

circle of chairs. "I have no intention of running all over Envoy Kearns' house like a child. Those actions are simply rude."

"You are correct, Commodore." Laurel crossed the room to stand in front of the overbearing officer. "As Kage is like a brother to me, I'm sure he will not mind if we limit our search to the hall, salon, parlor, and dining room."

"I still have no intention of participating." Commodore Pembrooke crossed his arms.

"Perhaps you could be 'it' for the first round? I'm sure a man with your experience and respect for the Envoy's home would be able to pick the perfect object and hiding place," she continued before he could protest.

"Humph. I suppose," he replied, seemingly resigned to his fate.

"Then I will not get to play." Sophia pouted.

"I will gladly search along with you, my dear," Aaron said in a soothing voice. "With the permission of the Commodore, of course?"

"Fine. Fine." Commodore Pembrooke replied. The man surveyed the room. Perhaps he was already searching for an object or hiding place.

"In the spirit of getting to know you, Mademoiselle Augustine, would you care to be my partner?" Count Pierre Jean asked. He took a bow between the two chairs opposite the coffee table. The man extended his hand with such flourish and style. Did he know how silly his gesture was? Dominique would have to go around the table to take his hand.

Dominique looked up at Raven and he nodded his assent before escorting her around the table to her new partner. Either the two were not as romantic as they let on at The Horizontal, or perhaps they didn't mind sharing. Laurel still speculated about their dynamics. Lost in thought, she hadn't paid attention to Raven crossing towards her. She realized her error too late.

"Lady Gunn would you do me the honor of being my—" Raven was cut off by a hard shove from her husband. Ben stood between them, facing Inspector Clarke.

"Benjamin Gunn!" She cuffed him on the shoulder.

"If anyone is going to partner with you, it should be me. You've been hinting at forming an alliance all night with the subtlety of an elephant twirling a flaming baton," he turned and practically snarled at her.

"I didn't." Laurel denied.

"You did," Ben said less harshly. "Unless you didn't mean what you said." His fingers slid sensuously over her bare arm.

"Oh, I meant every word, you stupid man," she whispered. Laurel couldn't resist the pull of this man and reached out to touch his cheek.

"Well, I guess partners are settled," Raven said.

The moment was broken and Laurel pulled back her hand.

"I guess you don't get to play," Sophia said to Raven.

"Miss, I'm an inspector; I don't need any hindrance from a partner. Now shall we adjourn to the dining room so we may begin? After you, Pembrooke." Inspector Raven Clarke ushered Commodore Pembrooke forward.

The Commodore walked on expecting the guests to follow him like soldiers in battle.

"Are the rest of you coming or are you going to gawk at the married couple," Raven called over his shoulder. The guests scattered from the room, like misled marching soldiers, orderly but with no sense of where to go.

Ben offered Laurel his arm.

She accepted it.

"You think they'll notice if we sneak away into the garden?" He asked.

Laurel stumbled. "There is no garden."

"Tsk, tsk. That is really too bad," Ben whispered before nibbling on Laurel's earlobe.

Too bad indeed.

* * *

INSPECTOR RAVEN CLARKE couldn't believe this stroke of luck. He could investigate at least this portion of the Embassy, and watch the guests for signs of suspicious activity. He was perfectly happy to search alone.

He was now free to search out clues to this new land, and perhaps decide what sort of man Envoy Kage Kearns truly was behind closed doors.

The others searched the agreed-upon rooms for the item that Commodore Pembrooke moved. Using his observations he deduced the mystery object was a small brass elephant serving as a tea kettle. He had read a plaque beside the kettle indicating it was inspired by the Jumbos offering transport about the city.

Raven observed Pierre Jean whispering in Dominique's ear as if they were already lovers sharing secrets. He would allow Dominique to win over the Frenchman. Her tactics would yield better results, and for the count to form an attachment to Dominique would benefit their cause.

Aaron and Sophia were the only couple searching for the object. Although, Raven suspected perhaps Aaron was avidly pursuing Miss Ostwalt and the young lady was cleverly avoiding his advances. No surprise.

Raven couldn't imagine Commodore Pembrooke would approve.

Ben and Laurel were missing from his perusal, however. Where had those two gotten off to?

* * *

BEN GRABBED Laurel's hand and pulled her along the narrow corridor leading to Kage's wine cellar. They moved downward until the light could no longer catch them. She was familiar with the room, as she and Kage traded wine back and forth.

"What are you doing?" She tried ineffectively to pull her hand away from him and retreat out the door. This small space enhanced her awareness of him and it wouldn't do to be caught making love in an envoy's house.

He effectively closed it behind her. "You've been driving me mad all night." He trailed kisses along her throat.

"Ben...I...." Laurel leaned back into the wine rack to balance, spreading her thighs slightly, should he want to venture lower. When it came to Ben, she had all the willpower of a child in a sweet shop.

His right hand trailed over her corset, down over her skirt. He grabbed the curve of her hip and pulled her against him.

"Ben, come home with me." Her voice pleaded against his ear before she planted her own kisses against his skin. She wanted their love behind closed doors where she could protect him from gossip and foreign agents who might report back to the royals.

"I can't."

She pulled back, "Why not?"

"It's not safe." At her bewildered look, he clarified, "For you. I'm not safe."

"Ben, whatever are you going on about? You make absolutely no sense." She pressed her question, even as she maintained the small distance between them. He truly believed he was protecting her. They really needed to talk.

* * *

"LAUREL, let your questions cease. Please, give me this?" Ben had managed to gather her skirt in his hand, exposing her lace-covered flesh beneath the tent. He ran his hand along the waist of her white bloomers. This style laced behind her. "Why are you wearing so many garments?"

"Do you not remember how to undo such things?" she asked coyly, her tongue darted across the seam of his lips.

"Oh, I remember, wife. I simply shouldn't have to do such things after many years of marriage."

"If you would come home with me, we could both undress, lay in an actual bed and you could do unspeakable things to me and my delicate bits…" her voice trailed off in a sing-song sort of way which tortured him.

"Be damned." He muttered against her skin and retrieved a knife from his pocket. He tugged the material, hoping for a rip and to free the delicate bits he wanted access to. No such luck. He took the knife in his left hand and pulled Laurel close to him; he cut the laces at her back. The cotton material fell in a white puddle on the floor. The victory was his and he intended to claim his prize.

Ben dropped to his knees before Laurel. He longed for a look at the dark blond curls at the apex between her legs. Truthfully, he didn't simply want a look; he craved the taste of her. The very heat of her had teased him from the moment Ben recalled every delectable tryst of their past. Ben recalled every moment of his wife squirming beneath him before he pleasured her, and himself.

Ben lifted her buttocks in his hands, tilting her hips towards him. He was overwhelmed by her feminine form.

"Benjamin…" she blurted out, stopping the moment.

"For God's sake woman, let me taste you. Pleasure you. A taste is all I want. My tongue on your flesh is all you should want." Ben raised his voice and spoke quickly. He couldn't hold his annoyance back. He wanted her too much.

* * *

LAUREL SURRENDERED. What choice did she have? This man wasn't a stranger, this was her husband. A man whom she heartily missed. A man whose very existence made her heart beat a bit faster and the air in her lungs a bit easier to take in. This man held the very lifeline to her soul. How could she deny him? Her choice wasn't a decision as much as the acceptance of what was hers to take.

Laurel leaned her head back and lifted her foot to rest on the tiniest of ledges, wedging her boot between bottles. The tiny ledge would have to do.

"Oh yes, my heart. Open wide for me." Despite the command, his voice was warm, like a fire dancing over her skin.

Laurel did as he bid. He paused, perusing her delicate self. Perhaps there had been others, women who were younger, or prettier, and pure. She wasn't truly aware of her husband's prowess until she trained as a courtesan. Only then did she realize what a truly gifted and bizarre specimen he was.

His silence continued.

"Paint a picture, it will last longer…" she muttered, wishing he would get on with it.

"I may do just that, wife. Do you have any idea what the mere sight of your female flesh does to me? It's an assault on my senses. My eyes behold the dark curls, shaped like a heart above your cunni. However, did you manage such a trick? It is truly lovely. My nose smells the musky scent you possess and I can't resist reaching my tongue out for a taste. Will your flavor be the same? Will age have done your juice justice like a wine? And of course, my fingers long to assail you."

Ben showed her what his touch could do. He ran his index and middle finger over her stocking to the top. His fingers traced along the edge, curling around and grasping the lace. He threatened to pull the stockings to her knees.

Before she could comment on the wrenching of her stockings, those same fingers skimmed along the crease of her folds. Laurel knew she was dripping with want. She practically hummed.

He teased his finger along the seam of her sex.

Laurel tilted her hips towards him, feeling the pressure of his digits entering her. A tiny cry passed her lips.

"Shh, wife," Ben removed his digits from her. "You'll get us found out."

Laurel bit her lip.

"Good Girl." He commented.

Ben slid his fingers back inside. She welcomed the roughness against the smooth walls of her tender flesh. He performed a dance with fine, restrained, rotating movements. Laurel arched into his exploring hand, and he increased the tempo. This was a dance they performed before and the pagan rhythm always assaulted her very soul. Ben's fingers grew warmer and felt longer the deeper into her canal he stroked. Ben continued his assault, letting Laurel reach her climax, shaking on the edge of infinity.

Ben drew up along her slender body, before sucking his fingers into his mouth, apparent joy on his face as he tasted her essence.

"My turn," he said. His voice was unbending, yet mysteriously gentle.

Before Laurel could drop to her knees at his command, they heard noises beyond the tunnel.

"Perhaps another time, my heart," Ben spoke before his swift exit. He left Laurel to retrieve her drawers and what remained of her decorum.

CHAPTER ELEVEN

Raven rounded the corner to find Laurel emerging from a curved passageway. She approached with such force, she collided with his chest. He grasped her firmly around the waist, trying to steady her.

Laurel reeled backward, stumbling away from him until her spine flattened against the limestone.

"Are you well?" he asked.

"Yes. I am in good health." She spoke hastily, before asking, "Have you seen Ben?"

"I have not."

Laurel gave him a quizzical look, before continuing, "I seem to have lost him, during our search."

"You may call off the search. Lieutenant March and Miss Ostwald found the object. It was a tiny elephant tea kettle."

"Oh yes!" She said with an enthusiasm that didn't reach the curve of her lips or her dark eyes. "The Jumbo kettles – they were given to all the Ambassadors by the Transport Bureau when the new pachyderms came online. I must congratulate the winning team." Laurel scampered back towards the parlor before Raven could stop her.

He peered down the shadowed corridor. How was she able to navigate through the darkness by herself? Perhaps she had been hiding inside the door. Why?

Raven took cautious steps down the corridor. He held his breath when the light was no longer available. Raven reached into his pocket for a match. He stopped, removing the match from its box and striking it along the stone wall. The match's burnished glow flickered against the damp dove gray walls. Raven scanned the scant light between the shadows for a lantern or other light source. Above his head, a row of candle sconces jutted out like sleeping sentries in the gloom. He reached and tugged one from its post. When the flame was about to touch his fingers, he touched the match to the wick and the flame came to life with a reassuring little pop. Raven shook his hand and extinguished the match.

With newfound illumination, Raven scanned the limestone walls before he arrived at the end of the tunnel. On his left was a rack of bottles. The dust had been disturbed along the front of the rack as though a gentleman's coattails or a lady's sleeve had inadvertently swept the layer aside.

As Raven stooped to investigate, his nose picked up the musky smell of sex. His gaze was captured by an object on the ground, glinting in the flickering candlelight. The knife was unusual. The tip was sturdy and sharp, while the edge remained dull. There wasn't a handle to speak of; the tang was smooth and one with the blade. There was no grip, rendering the knife useless. He placed the knife in the inner pocket of his duster.

The dirt appeared disturbed as well, and he ran his fingers beneath the racks, the length of the floor, for any evidence left behind; he found nothing. Raven walked back to the sconce and snuffed the flame, returning the candle to its housing. He silently moved from the dark recesses towards the radiance of light.

* * *

LAUREL FOUND her way back to the front parlor where all the guests except Ben were gathered, preparing to leave. Her husband was gone.

"Has Doctor Gunn left us already?" she asked, hopeful she sounded unconcerned.

"I've not seen him," Aaron responded before planting himself at her side.

"Nor I," said the count.

"Shall I see you home, darling?" Aaron asked her.

"I will escort these lovely ladies. This will give us a chance to further our acquaintance, no, ma chérie?" Pierre Jean lifted Dominique's hand to his lips.

"That will be fine." Laurel quickly retrieved her jacket from the coat rack in the corner. She was nearly dressed, ready to escape when Inspector Clarke approached from the back of the house.

"Inspector, will you be joining them on the Jumbo back to The Horizontal?" asked Aaron.

Laurel didn't want him on the trip back. Bad enough Raven had witnessed her in such a state of immodesty, now to have him travel with her. She knew she could not bear his scrutiny or interrogation tactics on the way home.

"I believe I shall walk. I find those pachyderms very cumbersome." He strode towards the door.

"I shall join you." Aaron was already buttoning his uniform frock and following suit.

Laurel breathed a sigh of gratitude. She caught movement on the stairs and saw Victoria coming down the stairs, her nose was red, and her eyes were swollen. Damn it. In her distraction with Ben, she'd forgotten about Sophia's insensitive remark regarding Fatima's death.

"Victoria," Laurel rushed to meet her friend at the banister. "I'm so sorry. I should've sent you a word about Fatima immediately. I was caught up in my own events. I wasn't thinking clearly."

"Is it true?" Victoria asked

Laurel gave her a quizzical look.

"Molly was attacked too?"

"Yes, but she is fine and resting at home," Laurel assured her.

"She would've been safe if you hadn't given her the boot, Laurel." Victoria's voice was laced with bitterness.

"Yes, well those events cannot be undone. Tori, why don't you come by for tea tomorrow?" Laurel asked, hoping to mend some of the hurt.

"Will this be one of your secret teas?" A voice behind them asked.

Laurel abruptly turned to challenge Sophia Ostwald. The woman was a true nuisance.

"There is nothing secret about them. I have tea with guests, ladies who work for me, the staff, and friends." Laurel said, resting her hand protectively on Victoria's arm.

"Then you wouldn't mind if I joined?" Sophia asked.

Tori's arm tensed beneath Laurel's hand. Even though Laurel didn't want the nosy Prussian there, she didn't want to create gossip since the former maid held the more powerful ear of Commodore Pembrooke. "Not at all. We can discuss the names Tori will pick for her baby."

"That sounds lovely. I will join you tomorrow at four o'clock," Sophia announced before taking her velvet cloak from Commodore Pembrooke.

"Good evening, ladies." Commodore Pembrooke tipped his hat to them before ushering Sophia out the door.

"Tori?" Laurel turned to look at her friend.

"Yes?" Tori's voice was barely a whisper.

"Come by at three and we'll visit with Molly. I'll sneak you out the back and arrange another tea with Sophia."

"Madam." Dominique tapped Laurel's shoulder. Laurel saw nothing. So this one was magical as well.

"I'll be there in a moment, Dominique." Laurel turned back to the door, anticipating her party's departure. The count and Kage stood by the door talking, out of earshot.

"I overheard that woman's rudeness," Dominique whispered. "If I may be of assistance, please let me know."

Laurel looked Dominique over. The girl was ready to go. Her voice was soft, but her eyes bespoke knowledge and steel Laurel often prized at her 'secret' teas. "Yes. I believe you can help me a great deal, Miss Augustine."

* * *

BEN WANDERED the dark streets of Constantinople. He didn't know why he'd left. He was afraid to get caught with his wife – stupid, that. He could still hear her cry of pleasure drumming in his ears.

God, the taste of her lingering on his tongue drove him mad.

How could he flee trying to forget her? It was no mystery he ended up in front of The Horizontal.

He hungered for her with something akin to desperation. This need wasn't only for her body. His desire was the smell of her and the softness of her form snuggled against him in the night. Feminine comfort most men didn't appreciate, but the qualities that made her, made him want.

She helped him sleep. Always had. She chased away the demons which held him in their grip. Even before he'd seen the ravages of war, he'd had difficulty falling asleep. Once they'd married, he wasn't gripped by strange creatures invading the steady, calm and restful sleep. Always her, her warm presence, her calm breath against his skin, her almost magical ability to soothe his soul. If he was anxious, nervous, or terrified, she sensed the imbalance and righted him with her mere presence.

Laurel accompanied him to Crimea since she'd refused to be left behind, and he'd worried for her safety. Though her safety was his first concern when he volunteered, a part of him was relieved he wouldn't go alone.

Ben retreated back into the shadows. A brass pachyderm approached, whistling its arrival. He bumped into a figure behind him.

He pivoted on his heel, reaching for the knife in his boot. He inhaled sharply. Nothing – he'd left the blade in Envoy Kearns' wine cellar when he'd cut Laurel's laces. He swore under his breath.

"No need to get aroused, Doctor Gunn."

Ben couldn't make out any distinguishing features.

The figure was cloaked head to toe in black.

"What do you want?" he asked.

"You don't remember me."

"I don't know you." Ben stood his ground. He dared not reveal himself or this menace to Laurel across the cobbles.

"From Osiris." The voice was familiar and haunted him.

"What?" Ben peered at the figure. Familiarity tickled his mind. He struggled against it.

"You were always my favorite." A dark gloved hand touched his face. A small hand. Encased in satin.

Ben recoiled from the touch. It made him uncomfortable. So, intolerable was the stranger's touch; it forced him from the shadows into the light. Memories of a dark cell, his chest open came flooding forward. He turned reeling from the onslaught. He vomited in the gutter.

"Ben? Are you alright, mon ami?" Pierre Jean stood beside him.

"That woman." Ben pointed to the shadows where he'd emerged. Although he admitted the voice sounded hoarse, not feminine.

"There is no one, my friend. You have been drinking too much, I think." Pierre Jean put his arm around him to try and assist Ben to stand.

"I'm fine." Ben shook him off. "Where's Laurel?" He looked at the Jumbo expecting to see his wife.

"She and Miss Dominique are within her house. She is well, I assure you. Are you feeling well?" Pierre Jean scanned him with the best of intentions, but not the skill. "Let us get you l'elephant, no? Get you home safely."

"No, thank you. I need some fresh air."

"I will walk with you then." Pierre Jean clearly was not leaving him alone.

"Fine." Ben resigned to his fate. He let the count walk next to him.

They walked in silence for many minutes before Ben asked, "How are your efforts at wooing Miss Augustine coming along?"

"Passably well, I think." Pierre Jean stood a bit straighter. He looked more confident if that was possible for the Frenchman.

Ben smiled.

"Her father was a Union commander. Dominique understands war and loss. It surprises me for a woman so beautifully hopeful and yet she saw much tragedy." Pierre Jean shook his head.

"America is still young. They are fresh from their civil war. The country will have to endure many growing pains."

"Oh ho, you speak as if you are not an American? This I know is not true." Pierre Jean stopped in front of Ben.

"I admit, with an English wife and schooling abroad, I feel more affinity with Great Britain," Ben confessed.

"Your wife is very attractive, for an Englishwoman," Pierre Jean ribbed him.

"I'm sure she'd say the same of you," Ben countered.

"There you are, *mon ami*." Pierre Jean slapped him on the shoulder. "I was worried about you, seeing strange things in the dark. The nightmares start before you go to sleep, no?"

"Not usually," Ben recalled Pierre Jean had been assigned to the same tent when they were stationed in India. "Ever since I've come to this city, I've had visions."

"What visions?" Pierre Jean asked

"Not war or anything you'd expect. They are things that are unfamiliar to me. Castles, cells with bars, wings like a bat, fire."

"Are they perhaps from your childhood? Your time at the circus?" Pierre Jean probed further. Ben glanced and he noted the concern etched in his friend's features.

"My father was a fire-eater and swallowed swords. This fire seems all-consuming like I was in it."

"Perhaps the dream is foreshadowing, or has a deeper meaning?"

Ben smiled. While Pierre Jean's father was of noble birth, his mother was of Hungarian descent, rumored to have been a gypsy. His friend had always been superstitious and fascinated by otherworldly things. Ben, having seen the cons of magic growing up, held no such mysticism.

"It is good we have arrived. I don't want to spend my time dispelling your belief." Ben turned to Pierre Jean to wish him goodbye.

"If you and Moody desire to stay in my flat, so you are safe, do not hesitate to call on me." Pierre Jean tipped his top hat to Ben, before walking into the shadows.

Ben stood silently staring at the rooftops. He couldn't help but feel eyes watching him. Before he could examine the sensation, the door opened behind him.

"Are you coming in, Doctor Gunn?" Moody asked.

"Yes. I thought I saw something," he replied.

Moody scanned the scenery behind Ben, as well as the rooftops across the street. "Best come in, sir. You can never be too safe."

CHAPTER TWELVE

"I think once the scar heals, it will add an element of mystery to your person," Victoria spoke before sipping her tea.

Laurel was glad Molly and Victoria were able to join her for a private tea this morning in 'Victoria's Room.'

"I suspect it will be a long time between disgust and mystery," Molly commented.

"What is most important is that you are alive and on the mend," Laurel interjected. "If you never work as a courtesan again it will not be the end of the world."

Molly raised an eyebrow at her.

"Why don't we plan a recital of sorts for you?" Victoria said

"A recital?" Molly raised her other eyebrow, before taking a cautious sip.

"Yes. I could reserve the theater at the Embassy and you could reveal your hidden talents." Victoria stood and paced the room. She tapped her chin with her index finger and looked thoughtful.

Molly choked on her tea and stood to face Victoria. "What talent do you intend to have me display?"

"Why your violin, of course." Victoria turned and faced Molly. "Molly, I'm an upstanding citizen now, I would never have you display your wares, especially on stage. Whatever kind of person do you think I am?" Victoria had an upward tilt to her mouth.

"You little minx, I could not imagine what you had in store for me."

Molly placed her hands on her hips and moved to stand in front of Victoria Tori.

Both young ladies broke out into giggles before collapsing on the bed.

Laurel cleared her throat. "Since we have Molly's debut performance in hand, I do have business matters to discuss."

True to form, Victoria and Molly sat up, all humor removed from their faces. Victoria stood and smoothed her skirts before she sat on the chest at the foot of the bed. For the Tea, she wore an emerald green robe with a lavender underskirt. The robe was covered in brocade flowers. Her wedding ring was displayed on her left hand with matching onyx earrings dangling from her ears. It was a definite stark contrast to the English gowns she used to wear. Victoria seemed to embrace the Arabian culture of her husband.

Molly, who was dressed much more informally, seated herself by the headboard and crossed her legs.

Laurel remained settled on the small chair during all their arrangements. "I'm very worried about Fatima's death and the attempt on Molly's life may be related to my teas."

"You mean you're spying." Not one to mince words, Molly barreled right to point like a bull in a china shop.

"Yes, that too," Laurel conceded.

"The teas apparently were not much of a secret," Victoria spoke up. "Miss Ostwald knew all about them."

"That prissy maid?" Molly asked.

"Yes, exactly the one," Laurel said.

"Do you think she's told Emory Pembrooke?" Victoria asked.

"I am not sure. I think her presence is even more reason we should give a performance when she arrives for tea," Laurel said.

"You invited her?!" Molly's voice rose to a level perhaps only slightly lower than a canine might hear.

"She invited herself," Victoria commented.

"What kind of performance did you have in mind?" Molly asked.

"Well, as Victoria stated, others may already be aware of the teas. There is no reason to believe my private teas are related to anything specific. Perhaps, we are all simply friends."

"This is true." Victoria nodded in agreement. "It's not as if we've revealed the magic behind closed doors.

"Maybe our friendship is why we were targeted because we are close to you?" Molly looked down, studying the pattern on the bedspread.

"No." Laurel hated to think her only allies were targeted because they were close to her. The belief that her own government would trap her as a madam at The Horizontal was not a comfort. Were her friends being killed because Queen Victoria learned that Laurel had been keeping her own secrets and allies? Could they suspect she was trying to leave, that she was seeking out humans with magic? Laurel didn't believe it. Laurel's father had ensured a lifetime of servitude so she was certain the queen wouldn't kill an asset. Besides, she would've been taken out directly, not those around her. No one defied the Queen and lived. Perhaps the magic Laurel sensed in each of the women was the reason. Fatima sensed the future. Victoria read tea leaves and Molly could see the dead. They weren't fae but humans with magic.

"I thought Fatima was killed by The Cleaver?" Victoria questioned.

"Yes," replied Molly. "As far as I know The Cleaver is a madman and not known to have any ties to anyone political or otherwise."

"I believe the killing was random, not necessarily tied to The Horizontal or myself. And I certainly don't believe the queen has hired a madman to begin killing gypsies and witches." Laurel assured them.

Both women gave her dubious looks.

"Enough of this somber conversation, Let's discuss this afternoon's tea." As always Laurel believed the less they knew the safer they should be. She'd never had any reason to reveal her true nature and let them believe her to be a powerful witch.

"I will be there since she witnessed you inviting me," Victoria said vehemently.

"I will be there as well," Molly insisted.

"Molly, I'd prefer you to stay in your rooms," Laurel said.

"You don't trust me." Molly pouted.

"That's not true," Laurel assured her. "I do have a question, however."

"Yes?"

"I know you and Aaron were close. Did you ever tell him about the teas, or how we divined information for Queen Victoria?"

"No." Molly looked down seemingly fascinated with the quilt again.

"I know you and he were close," Laurel stressed the words again before pressing her lips shut.

"You're wonderin' if I betrayed you," Molly asked. "If I told him about your boards of dying men, Fatima's crystal ball, or Victoria agreeing based on the leaves in the bottom of the cup?"

"Yes." Laurel needed to know the truth.

"I did not," Molly answered with a ferocity Laurel hadn't known she still possessed in her recovering condition. "I cannae reveal them without revealing myself, can I? Did you ask Tori if she told Kage?"

"She did," Victoria lied.

Laurel stiffened and her eyes widened on Victoria. She left the lie alone. There would be time to talk to Victoria later.

"Alright, let us move on, shall we?" Laurel put all further arguments to a halt and they discussed their upcoming ruse. She wondered if The Cleaver wasn't motivated by politics. Perhaps he was motivated by magic. Fatima also had a gift for reading people. Whether by magic or simply good intuition, Laurel was not sure. Perhaps she divined the Clreaver's true identity and that knowledge led to her death.

* * *

LAUREL FINISHED POURING tea at her table when Sophia commented on her guest's attire.

"That is an interesting outfit for tea," Sophia nodded toward Dominique.

"I have to work following our tea," Dominique responded smoothly. Dominique Augustine wore an eggshell white shirt and satin black corset, with black pantaloons and fishnet stockings. An ebony bustle and ermine collar completed her outfit. Laurel would've expected this type of wear if the girl was working the floor, but not for tea. Well, she was at fault for not warning Dominique.

"I was glad Dominique could join us before starting her shift. These teas have always been rather informal. I don't stand on ceremony like Mother England." Laurel confirmed.

"I used to dress more formally myself," said Victoria.

"I didn't realize your 'secret' teas were close to working hours," Sophia commented. Sophia was probably the most traditionally dressed for tea. She wore a fitted lace top covering her from neck to wrist, with a camisole sheath. On her head, was a straw hat with matching lace around the band with a peach ribbon. The ribbon matched her corset and skirt. She wore flowered armored wristbands which matched the brooch at her throat. A pocket watch at the top front closure of her corset completed her outfit.

"I don't know if they are secret. I've held a tea during The Horizontal's opening hours, it depends on each girl's individual schedule and if they are available. I even have tea with the staff. Had you cared to stay on, you would have known this," Laurel retorted.

"Perhaps, but I believe I have a much better arrangement," Sophia replied before taking a sip of her tea.

"Indeed! How is Commodore Pembrooke as a lover?" Victoria asked bluntly.

Dominique laughed into her cup.

Laurel bit her lip to keep a modicum of decorum.

"I don't know what you are talking about." Sophia shifted in her chair. Color to shame her father's roses flared on the Prussian's cheeks.

"Oh, come now," Victoria continued. "Are you not living in his house, attending every social event with him?"

"Yes, but we—"

"Posh," Victoria waved her hand at Sophia's denial. "We are all adults here, and have done illicit things with the men of this city."

"God bless the men and their needs," said Dominique.

"Cheery-Oh," Victoria sailed on. "If it weren't for those needs, I would not find myself married to one of Constantinople's most influential politicians."

"You, you were a prostitute!" exclaimed Sophia.

"We prefer the term courtesan," interjected Laurel, hoping to smooth things over, before Sophia insulted the present company.

"I worked in this very establishment," Victoria said. "This is where Kage and I met."

"Of course, my brother wanted Tori almost exclusively once she arrived from Great Britain," Laurel vowed to show Sophia there was nothing suspicious to be found.

"Brother?" Sophia looked from Victoria to Laurel puzzled.

"Envoy Kage Francis Kearns was raised in the Sultan's palace where I trained. Didn't you know that?" Laurel asked

"I—"

"Perhaps if you had stayed..." Dominique reminded Sophia before taking a coconut macaroon off the china plate in the middle of the table.

"Perhaps I should return," Sophia suggested

"There is no need. You are well established as a mistress, which is the goal of The Horizontal," Victoria said.

"It is?" Sophia asked.

"Of course," Dominique said. "It's why I came all the way from the Americas. I wanted to find a rich benefactor." The American was playing along very well. Laurel would have to watch her carefully and see if she could pull this one into her fold.

"Why would you come from America to Constantinople?" Sophia sounded suspicious.

"European men are more willing to take a woman such as me as their mistress."

"Not in the United States?" Victoria asked. "They seem modern without their hierarchy of lords, counts, and barons."

"Maybe it is our youth as a country, or perhaps the Civil War and the costs of it. There is not much money found among men who would perhaps marry outside their race." Dominique seemed to choose her words carefully.

"Is your goal marriage?" asked Sophia.

"Not so much marriage, as much as the stability a man of wealth and prestige can offer. You of all people should understand this," Dominique said.

"Which brings me back to my question, how is Commodore Pembrooke as a lover?" Victoria asked.

"I do not know," Sophia responded.

"Oh come now, Sophia, do not be coy," Victoria insisted.

"I live in his house, have my own room, and attend events as his companion. The man has not taken me as his lover." Sophia clutched her teacup in one hand and splayed her other over her heart.

"That is most odd." Victoria grabbed another cookie from the tray.

"Mayhap he prefers men," Dominique proposed. "It is not an uncommon thing."

"Do you think?" Victoria asked.

"It is not possible. Look at me," Sophia protested, seemingly troubled by the turn of conversation.

"You are simply a ruse..." Dominique eyed Sophia up and down as if judging her and deciding the girl's appearance was why Commodore Pembrooke did not want the lovely Prussian.

"There may be another reason," Laurel interrupted.

"Yes?" Sophia asked, leaning forward awaiting an answer.

"Commodore Pembrooke is an older man. He may not perform as often as his younger counterparts or even have the desire," Laurel suggested, hoping to salvage the young woman's false modesty.

"I don't recall him ever attending The Horizontal," Victoria said.

"Oh, he wouldn't," Laurel clarified.

"Why?" asked Dominique.

"He's a member of the Church of the Holy Alliance, and follows their strict doctrine," Laurel said.

"Then my living with him is not so bad," Sophia spoke up. "At least I am with a respectable religious man." She held an air of superiority acting like she was above those around her.

"There is that, but where is the fun?" Victoria winked at her.

"Indeed." Dominique stood and stepped lightly around the other ladies toward the doorway. "I'm afraid I must find a man in search of such fun."

"Perhaps not for very much longer," Laurel commented. "Count Pierre seems very interested in you. He may ask for an exclusive contract like Kage did with Victoria."

"A girl can only hope," Dominique said. She nodded at the ladies before taking her leave.

"I thought perhaps she arrived with that inspector gentleman," Sophia said.

"She did. He escorted her across the seas. I believe her father paid him to see to his daughter's safety." Laurel had no idea if the story was true, but it sounded reasonable.

"A father sending his daughter into prostitution, it seems rather deplorable," Sophia commented.

"It does, doesn't it?" Laurel couldn't agree more. Her own father committed such an act. Of course, hadn't her mother been sold like cattle to her father? Thanks to the Queen, her father was now a country gent. What did his parishioners think? Did he yet have a parish? Likely he abandoned religion altogether, once he'd gained his title.

"I'm sure finding a husband is what Dominique wants." Victoria gave Laurel a darting glance.

"I'm sure it is," Laurel agreed. "I can't see someone as independent as Dominique agreeing to something simply because her father chose it."

"Well, we are not all given choices," Sophia said.

Perhaps Sophia was under similar circumstances, where she had lost a father and was forced into such things.

"That is true when my own father died, my stepmother wanted me gone immediately. Laurel's own father negotiated the deal for me to come here."

"Your father is a flesh peddler?" Sophia asked, clearly aghast.

Laurel didn't mince words "No, my father merely traded my flesh for a title. I'd like to say all my girls came here willingly like Dominique and Molly. Some have no choice and others are sold into this life. Usually, when those things happen, I try to find roles they'd prefer in the house. Not everyone has what it takes to work on their backs."

"Speaking of backs, mine is starting to ache," Tori said. Standing, she straightened her shoulders.

"I'll go with you." Sophia rose to leave.

Laurel watched the two women leave. While she had learned a bit more about Sophia's relationship with Commodore Pembrooke, other questions arose. Sophia's motives remained a mystery.

CHAPTER THIRTEEN

*D*octor Gunn stood over his desk, looking at the fibers through the microscope. They were not his, nor anything human he recognized. The hairs looked as if shed from a beast.

Possibly some sort of fur from a coat dropped at the scene contaminating Fatima's body, but the only creatures surrounding her form were the dodos and their samples were feather-like.

"Moody!" He called out.

"Yes, sir?" Moody was at the archway of Ben's lab as if Ben had conjured the young man's arrival.

"Have you ever seen a hair like this?" He stood back and motioned for Moody to look at the fibers on the slide.

Moody stepped forward, set his book on the counter, and adjusted the settings to better suit him. "Looks like animal fur?"

"Yes, I thought so, too. I thought maybe something local?" Ben asked.

"Nothing I know of sir." Moody reached for his book.

"I can't say I know a lot about furs, despite having been surrounded by circus animals most of my life, except maybe bears. Wait!" Ben nudged Moody out of the way. "It might be bear fur."

"Bear? We have no bears here," Moody stated as a matter of fact before looking up.

"Are you certain?" Ben peered again at the sample. Guard hairs on a bear were about the length of this particular strand.

"Yes." Moody seemed absorbed in his studies rather than paying attention to the conversation at hand.

"I'm not aware of any with bluish-black fur anyway." Ben closed his eyes. He was no closer to finding Fatima's killer than when Inspector Raven retrieved him days ago. He must identify the threat posed to The Horizontal and more importantly Laurel.

A bell sounded above their heads, indicating someone arrived outside the door.

"I'll get it, Doctor." Moody scrambled away to answer the door. He came back a few minutes later with Inspector Raven Clarke in tow. The inspector wore his typical uniform of black. He was coated in darkness from his Stetson hat down to his cowboy boots. His face was barely visible beneath a dark kerchief covered in sand.

"Inspector," Ben greeted him.

"Doctor," Raven acknowledged, removing the scarf from his mouth.

"What brings you back to my office, on such a dark and windy night?" Ben asked.

"I think you should come back to The Horizontal," Raven said.

"Did Laurel send you?" Ben asked. He recalled her invitation to stay in her bed. Had she sent the inspector to do her bidding?

"No. I found something at Envoy Francis Kearns's house, which I thought might interest you," Raven said

"Oh?" Ben asked

"Yes, a weapon." Raven reached into his pocket.

"Do you believe it belongs to the Cleaver?" Ben asked.

"I'm not sure. What do you think?" Raven pulled the object out, revealing Ben's knife.

Ben's jaw stiffened. He berated himself. Ben had left the blade behind during his passionate encounter with Laurel and it was found by the Inspector. He didn't bother to deny it, "It's mine."

"So, you were in the cellar with Laurel," Raven spoke as if puzzling pieces together in his head.

"I was. She is, after all, my wife."

"And she was breathless because?" Raven asked, leadingly.

Ben knew what the Inspector was trying to get at. "Why, is none of your damn business."

Raven laughed.

"What do you find humorous, man?" Ben asked.

95

"You. I don't care what dalliances you had with your wife. There is no way your blade did the damage the Cleaver has done. It is far too blunt, except for the point. It's an odd knife for a doctor to carry around, a scalpel perhaps, but not this crude excuse for a knife. What kind of blade is it?"

"A circus knife, for throwing." Ben took the dagger from Raven and demonstrated it by throwing it at a corkboard along the back wall of his laboratory.

"Throw knives much, do you?" Raven asked.

"Not for many years now," Ben assured him. "Is this all you wanted to see me about? I'm very busy and don't have time to satisfy your every curiosity."

"I was wondering if you had found any additional clues on Fatima," Raven asked.

"Nothing new, I'm afraid. I have however found many unusual clues from Miss Molly Flannigan though."

"Molly Flannigan?"

"The Cleaver's second victim," Ben stated. Had Raven lost his wits?

"I hadn't heard of a second corpse."

"No, you wouldn't. She managed to live."

"Where is she?" Raven asked

"She's staying at The Horizontal," said Ben.

"The devil you say. Right under my nose!" Raven said.

"Calm down. I doubt my wife is going to let you interrogate a victim. Especially one she considers her responsibility to protect."

Raven sighed. "You're correct. What can you tell me about the weapon?"

"Well it's like a scalpel," Ben said.

"This information doesn't bode well for you, doctor."

"True. However, the blade is much larger, both in length and width. The precision of the cuts are too perfect for an amateur. If the man is not a doctor, I would be damned surprised."

"Again, this is not good. You put yourself at the top of my suspect list," Raven said.

"Why would I give you this information if I was The Cleaver?" Ben asked. He wanted to find the truth, for Laurel's safety. Even if he was revealed to be the killer.

"Perhaps to throw me off my trail," Raven said.

"Why not place me in cuffs then?" Ben asked.

Raven shrugged."You love your wife. I can't imagine you'd do anything to harm her. I can see why you two are married."

"Can you now?" Ben speculated on the true meaning behind the inspector's motives.

"Absolutely, the constant banter and side glances. As I'm not in the middle of your squabble, I find it all quite amusing."

"Good for you." Ben didn't bother to hide his sarcasm.

"It does make me wonder…" Raven paused, struggling to complete his thought. "If perhaps your lovely wife might be in danger."

"How so?" Ben's pulse raced and he could've sworn he felt his bones shift slightly at the mere mention of Laurel in danger.

"The Cleaver's latest victims both worked for Laurel. Do you not question if perhaps your wife may be the next intended target?" Raven asked.

"To be honest, I hadn't thought much beyond Fatima and Molly, examining them to find the true nature of this beast among us." Ben practically spit out the words. He replayed the night of Fatima's death in his head. He remembered the blood on his hands and the heart now soaking in formaldehyde. Had he attacked Molly too? He averted his gaze from the inspector, not willing to reveal his perfidy.

"Do not fret, doctor. We shall work together. Your job is to determine how these women were killed. Mine is to find out why. And not to worry if you are the villain, I will place you in cuffs, despite any of your wife's protests." The Inspector's words did not comfort Ben. If anything he was even more adamant to make sure Laurel was safe and an end put to The Cleaver once and for all.

"Doctor, I must be off. I will see if I cannot speak with this Molly. I will let you know our next course of action." Raven turned to leave.

"Wait! I'm coming with you. If you plan to interrogate Molly, you'll need someone to distract my wife."

* * *

LAUREL STOOD AT THE BAR, drink in hand, scanning the area for trouble. She tipped her head to the side and her heart raced when her husband walked in with Inspector Raven Clarke. She had a feeling Ben would seek her out. He seemed to be searching the room. For her? She felt a ripple of excitement. Ben looked rather smart in his tan trousers, tweed jacket, and leather gloves matching the leather of his shoes and the straps on his goggles. He still carried a cane with an ivory-carved handle in the shape of a dragon. Once his dark green eyes locked on hers, she sauntered over to greet him.

"Doctor Gunn, can I find you a woman to warm your bed?" She slowly sipped her scotch.

"Yes." His smile was slow and sensual.

Laurel was dumbfounded. How dare he seek respite within her premises.

"You will do fine, wife," his eyes filled with fierce possession.

"I beg your pardon." She sputtered. Backing up she coughed and grasped the rail going to the stairs above. Clutching her heart, she took deep breaths. She struggled to find balance. Everything was within her grasp and yet she mistrusted her good fortune.

"Are you all right?" Ben asked before placing his strong hand on her back to steady her.

"I'm fine." Laurel shook off his touch and shooed him away with her free hand. She stood straight. "What changed your mind?" She had to know before they proceeded any further. Why had he come to her?

"I'm worried for your safety. I agree it is best if you have someone to guard you."

"The Inspector and Omar can handle the job." She nodded to where the two men sat playing cards in the library. She didn't want his obligation. She wanted something far more valuable.

"Nonetheless, as your husband, I feel I must protect you."

"Duty!" Laurel fumed. It seemed with this man it was always half a step forward and two steps back. "I don't want your duty."

"What then?" Ben frowned and crossed his arms.

"I want your heart. It seems fair since you already have mine." Laurel whispered in desperation. If she had Ben's heart, together they could leave this place and start something new.

He reached his hand out and caressed her cheek. "Don't you know, Darling? You have it. You always have."

"Truly," Laurel's voice quieted. She'd been prepared for battle and yet her husband set her off-kilter. She searched his strong and rigid profile and saw a glimpse of the man she fell in love with.

"Laurel, come to me." Ben stretched out an arm towards her.

"No husband, you come with me." She grasped his hand and led him upstairs.

* * *

RAVEN GROANED as he stared down at one of the worst hands he'd had all evening. The Turk had won the last three games, much to the chagrin of those remaining at the table.

"Omar, have you no guilt? I have nothing in my pockets. What about my family?" Raven asked.

Omar looked at him and shrugged.

"Fine, what about Miss Augustine? What monies shall I give her for her talents?"

"Miss Augustine?" Omar lifted his head from his count.

Good, the man did have a conscience.

"She's fine." Omar nodded over Raven's shoulder.

Raven looked to the lounge. Dominique sat on the count's lap whispering in his ear. The man ran a finger under the top of her stocking.

"Well hell," Raven muttered under his breath.

"Perhaps you can spend time with Miss Molly? You were asking about her earlier." Omar nodded to the piano where Molly sat listening on a nearby bench.

"I think I will, Omar. I fold." Raven placed his cards face-down.

The other players groaned, likely knowing they were missing another easy win.

"Thank you." Raven stood and made his way to the red-haired beauty.

He slowed his pace and wound around the tables of patrons - playing cards, to arrive on her exposed side. He sat down.

She turned.

The first thing Raven noticed was her eyes. One green and one brown. Ghost Eyes the Chippewa called them.

"So, you see the dead?" He spoke without thought.

"What?"

"My people believe those with ghost eyes have one foot here and one in the afterlife. Some even see the dead."

"Who are you?" she asked, her brow furrowed.

"I'm sorry, Miss Flannigan. My name is Raven Clarke. I'm the inspector investigating Fatima's death."

Molly took a sharp breath.

"I understand you narrowly escaped The Cleaver yourself," he said.

"Yes." Her voice was hushed.

"Would you care to tell me about it? It may help us find Fatima's killer."

"Us?"

"Doctor Gunn and I have pooled our expertise to track down the villain," he clarified.

Molly sighed before telling Inspector Raven the events of the night.

"You say the creature had red eyes?" he asked when she was finished with her story.

"Yes. Why do you say creature?" she asked.

"I'm not aware of any man in the world who has red eyes. Even if a mad man did, there would perhaps be something unnatural about him."

Molly nodded in agreement.

"Is there anything else you can think of which may perhaps help?" he asked.

"I've spoken with Fatima," she said.

"Before she died?"

"After."

"So, you do possess the gift." He nodded for her to go on. "What did she say?"

CHAPTER FOURTEEN

Molly exhaled the breath she held. Never had someone readily accepted her gift. "You must not be from around here, sir."

"You are correct. I'm from 'across the pond' as you Brits say," he said.

"I'm Irish, but I'll forgive your ignorance. You are an American?"

"Yes."

"Are you a friend of Doctor Gunn's?"

"We've only met recently, but were brought together by these tragic circumstances."

"The Cleaver." Her stomach churned. She'd barely escaped the monster and now this stranger wanted to wreck her calm façade.

"Exactly," he maneuvered her over to a settee. "Can you tell me more about your conversation with Fatima?"

"The dead are not always forthcoming," she said.

At his puzzled look, she elucidated, "Spirits do not speak directly as you and I do."

"What were you able to infer from your communication?"

"She repeated one thing over and over." Molly stopped, shaking her head, and lowered her gaze. "I may be wrong about what it means..." she broke off with a sob.

"Tell me madam and we can weigh the significance of it," Raven took her arm and encouraged her to continue.

"She kept repeating Laurel's decree." Her hands trembled.

"Do you believe Laurel is somehow involved?" he asked.

"I can't believe Laurel would ever harm us. It is too far-fetched." She tried to conquer her reactions to that probing look of his.

"I understand you were not in residence when Fatima was attacked."

"Yes. I was staying in the Red Lamp district on the edge, near the desert." She recalled with frightening clarity.

"Do you believe your departure initiated the attacks?" he asked.

Molly wondered about her timing and the violence too. Perhaps the Brotherhood of the Veil had hired an assassin to eliminate her. Yet, it did not make sense for the Veil to attack Fatima or even Laurel's establishment. Even if they knew Fatima was a witch, The Brotherhood was more focused on Queen Morgan's plans to break free from the royal families.

"I don't believe so," was her response.

"Why did you leave?"

"Laurel gave me the boot." She spoke fast, she didn't bother to think. "She had her reasons, but we are presently reconciled." Molly quickly added.

"I see," he said.

Molly stared helplessly. He pulled from his jacket a small leather binder, flipped it open, and wrote within the pages.

"What are you writing?" she asked.

"Personal notes," he said. "Did Fatima have issues with anyone? Perhaps she had an altercation with Laurel, someone within the establishment, or outside these walls?"

"No," she shook her head. "The thing is, Fatima was well-liked by most one and all." Molly looked down at her lap.

"What are you keeping a secret, Miss Flannigan?" he asked.

"It is nothing." Dare she reveal Fatima's skill with a crystal ball or the tarot cards?

"Whatever it is, let me decide the significance of it." The Inspector's pen was poised to record Molly's every sin.

"Some of the gentlemen who frequent this establishment wanted Fatima to service them, not simply dance." She must tread carefully with this man. She did not know where his loyalties lie.

Inspector Clarke nodded, made a few notes, and gave her a probing look one more time. "Anything else you can think of?"

"No." Molly lifted her gaze and continued to stare following the Inspector's rise from the bench.

"If you think of anything, please don't hesitate to come to me for aid," he said before turning to go.

Molly had no chance to retreat to her rooms before she saw the Irish ambassador heading her way.

Seamus O'Grady was a barrel-chested leprechaun, with a mop of unruly carrot-colored hair. It looked rather like a seagull flew through it at random tearing tufts from his scalp. His hairline receded back from his forehead like the tide, leaving a barren stretch of skin as pock-marked and uneven as the rocky Irish coast. He wore a suit the color of a dun pony with black velvet trim on the collar and cuffs. His ensemble included a blood crimson-colored vest with a black ascot, pronouncing the stark white in his shirt. Dangling between a button and his vest pocket, a gold chain indicating he wore his pocket watch. An item he always had with him.

"Miss Flannigan." Ambassador O'Grady nodded his head before seating himself where Inspector Clarke recently vacated.

"Seamus." She smiled. No need for formalities, the man had already known her for years. Despite her loyalty to Laurel, she worked for Seamus and the Brotherhood of the Veil. The Brotherhood was charged with seeking out those with gifts, recruiting them to find magical objects, scrolls, or people. Molly had been recruited to spy on Laurel herself. Laurel's success at predicting death was unusual and considered unnatural.

"I'm glad to see you back here among friends," he said.

"Am I?" Molly didn't necessarily see it as such. Even though she was safe from The Cleaver, Laurel's house was not exactly safe. She was back in the fray of politicians and predators.

"Perhaps not, but we are in a risky business, you and me," O'Grady said.

Molly didn't deny it. She'd been in risky business all her life. She knew her days on this earth were numbered in the few. The most she could hope for was a simple death.

"I suppose your disfigurement will put a damper on the intelligence you can gather from your suitors." He stared pointedly at the bandage on her cheek.

"Who can say?" Looking around, she counted the number of tables she would need to move around to reach the staircase.

"Let's have a look." Without asking, Seamus leaned over and removed the dressing covering her cheek. "That is rather brutal-looking. I'm thinking perhaps if you keep it covered and are rutted in a fashion which doesn't require a man to look upon the jagged flesh, you can still be of use to us."

Molly pulled away as much from his words, as his touch. Her skin itched. Her fingers shook as she struggled to replace the bandage.

"Did he cut through the flesh? Can you still swallow a man?" Often, O'Grady would request her presence and after she had given her report to him, would make use of her services.

"The doctor said I'm not to resume my regular duties until I've fully recovered." She cast her eyes downward, determined not to reveal her joy.

"That is too bad. Who is your doctor?"

"Doctor Gunn. Laurel's husband."

"Ah, yes. The American returned from the dead."

Molly was not surprised he knew of the doctor's return. Seamus and other members of the Brotherhood made it a point to know what was going on inside Laurel's house.

"Who has been giving you the information in my absence?" she asked, wanting to set all the bits together. Molly had been feeding facts to them all along, except for the previous fortnight, while she was exiled.

"Be serious girl. You didn't think we would place simply one operative inside the queen's whorehouse, did you?" His self-satisfied sneer mocked her.

Molly stood taken aback. She was unsure of herself more than she'd ever been since she had aligned herself with Queen Morgan La Fae and the Brotherhood. She scanned the room. Who was this unknown accomplice? Had O'Grady's partner in crime fed information on her, on Laurel, on Fatima?

"Sit back down." Seamus reached out grabbing her arm. His face colored fiercely.

"I feel tired." She pulled and struggled for breath. She needed to escape this place and him. Did The Cleaver work for the Brotherhood? If Laurel was involved, did she know Molly had betrayed her? She trembled. Terrifying images built in her mind.

Seamus released her, and she fell backward with such force that she landed on her bottom. Patrons turned and stared.

Molly stiffened, momentarily mortified. Color stained her cheeks. She struggled to rise.

Seamus offered her his hand, but she waved him off.

Once on her feet, Molly fled up the stairs to the balcony, towards her room and safety.

CHAPTER FIFTEEN

*B*en followed his wife. She led him up the stairs to her private rooms. They passed briefly through her sitting room, where she'd served him tea the other day, to her bedroom.

"You're staying here," she said.

"Oh?" He was still stunned by his newly aggressive wife. The younger version of her had been timid. Timid wasn't the right word. She'd always been a hellion at least with her father. Perhaps he'd been fortunate to see her softer side. Was there any softness left in her, or had war and circumstances permanently removed his amenable wife?

"You don't necessarily have to stay in my rooms, but I would like you close at hand until this Cleaver business is over and the investigation of Fatima's death is resolved," she said.

"Don't you feel safe?" he asked.

"Oh, I feel safe enough with Omar here. I'm worried about your safety."

He gave a hollow laugh.

She sighed. "Fine. I'm tired of the distance between us. When you are near my soul aches." She sat on the bed running her fingertips over the covers.

Ben grew hard thinking of those very fingers on him. He lowered his head and gave her form a raking assessment. Though her head was down, her breathing was in little gasps. Was she breathless in anticipation of his next move?

He considered for a moment, all the delectable kisses he might place on her body. God, he wanted her. He worried instead of protection, he would bring danger. As he debated, her scent drifted to him. The slick wetness of enthusiasm was a potent aphrodisiac. "How can you want me, my heart?"

She lifted her head. "How can I not? Despite my profession, I've never felt the satisfaction I had with you."

Neither had he. The things he'd introduced her to, were pure animalistic rituals. Perhaps it was years in the circus or listening to boys brag about their sexual escapades. Maybe his desire was his own depravity which drove his lust beyond the bounds of nature.

"I've not played the games we played with another." She tempted him. Her enticement was unnecessary. His want for her was palatable.

"Stop." He lifted his hand.

Her mouth closed with a pout. Her bottom lip protruded

He longed to nibble the rosy bit between his teeth.

"You want to serve me?" He walked over and sat in her rocking chair.

"Yes."

"Remove your gown," he growled. The sexual beast that lay dormant had finally risen. The brute wanted nothing more than to feast on her flesh.

* * *

Laurel stood before him. Finally, the man who started her lessons of love had returned. The commanding tone in which he requested her servitude had her wet and craving fulfillment.

She removed her black velvet jacket. The smooth satin lining felt coarse along her sensitive skin. She tossed the coat to the bench at the end of her bed. Next, she removed her onyx-colored overskirt, letting the material puddle at her feet on the floor. She hadn't worn a bustle tonight so she stood in her royal blue corset, thin chemisette, stockings, and bloomers.

"Come here," Ben beckoned from the chair. The sparse rocker might as well be his throne.

She obeyed, walking short steps before she stopped before him. She closed her eyes awaiting his next command.

He buried his face against her abdomen and inhaled deeply. "I can smell you." He whispered against the fabric, before placing his fingers at the moistness between her legs. He rubbed them back and forth. The seam of the cloth teasing her sensitive bud nestled between her folds.

He stroked the linen back and forth rubbing her until she begged, "Please."

"What my heart?"

"May I remove them?"

"Why?"

Laurel knew better than to answer if she wanted his touch or him inside her, Ben would only torment her longer until she came to his terms. "So, you can feel how wet I am?" she answered.

His emerald eyes glowed with a primal fire. Yes, she recalled exactly what he wanted in the bedroom. "You are soaking the fabric, my heart. A spring of heat, wet, and scent." He inhaled sharply. He pushed the digit into her heat as well as the linen fabric.

Laurel gasped at the small fullness of fabric filling her.

He pushed back and forth the cloth-covered appendage until she was meeting the tiny yet satisfying thrusts of his finger.

"Yes," he said, pressing his nose toward where she most ached. Her husband was a predictable man at times.

"Damn it, Ben, why must you make me yearn before you have me?" She exhaled an agonizing moan.

He stood. His breath was hot against her ear, "Because I can."

No longer completely the submissive miss he married, Laurel lifted and buried her hands in his thick auburn hair before nibbling on his ear and whispering, "Who says I'll let you?"

Laurel buried her face against his throat and lightly nipped his flesh.

Ben pulled back parting them a few inches. He searched her face, staring into her eyes. "What happened to you?" His hands traced the laces along her back.

"I grew up. I'm no longer the fragile and absolute compliant girl you left behind." Though she longed for the protectiveness of Ben's arms, the daring and fortitude needed for survival lay beneath the surface. Her pretending otherwise was impossible.

His response was to swiftly cut the laces from her back allowing the corset to fall.

Through her gauzy chemisette, her breasts were revealed to his gaze. His mouth quickly followed. He licked circles around her tight nipples before drawing the fabric-covered tips between his teeth and sucking them.

"Oh, pull on them harder love," she demanded.

He pulled back. Lifting his gaze to hers, he said, "Grown-up indeed? How wonderful." He returned to his assault.

"If you keep this up, I will spend before you've even possessed me," Laurel warned him.

"Go ahead my dear, I don't mind. I'm not going anywhere." He spoke without arrogance.

His hand moved rhythmically against her. He nibbled and sucked at her breasts. The sensation was unbearable. His words released her, she dared not hold back.

Her inner muscles convulsed around his finger. She screamed against his throat. She rode waves of ecstasy.

He slowly removed his superb finger from the cleft between her legs.

She moaned at the loss. She had no desire to leave him and buried her face in his shirt.

His arms encircled her, his fingers curling beneath her arse. He lifted, and her trembling limbs clung to him.

* * *

BEN WAS SATISFIED BEYOND MEASURE. He loved the young and naïve wife of his youth. And yet the woman before him was a challenge. She engaged his senses and demanded his attention. His mouth fell open at her euphoric touch.

He shook off the fact her knowledge was gained perhaps through other lovers. Those men, and perhaps women, were in the past. Though her path may trouble him slightly, his doubt was not worth losing the prize. His wife was stronger and capable of accepting his deepest needs and darkest secrets.

As he carried her towards the bed, her soft curves molded to his hard contours. When they reached the edge, he set her down.

She unwound her arms from his neck, before loosening the ties on her chemisette. undid the buttons at her neck before pulling the now damp fabric over her head and tossing it to the floor.

He pushed her back watching her sink into the brocade silk covers.

She tried to rise.

He placed his hands on her shoulders, "No."

She looked at him quizzically.

"Let me enjoy the view of you." His voice was firm and his gaze fixed. She reclined, lifting her hands above her head. Laurel's normal golden honey skin held the rosy flush of arousal. Her breasts rose and fell. He touched the underside of the twin globes before bringing his fingers to her peaked nipples.

The color reminded him of peaches right before harvest. Ben couldn't resist plucking on the nipples.

Laurel moaned.

Ben's gaze drew below her navel following the curve of her hips, where she still wore the bloomers with a wet stain at the center between her legs. He was more than ready to remove the barrier.

He flexed his fingers and let his nails lengthen to rip the garment as he had her laces. At times there were advantages to releasing his beast. With his hands, he gripped the sides gathered at the top and split the fabric from her treasures.

Her cunni glistened wet and her flesh was bright pink. "Did the fabric chafe you?" He tried to sound calm but felt the beast shaming him for doing her harm.

"No, I'm simply flushed with want." She lifted her hips.

"Fine." His cock bucked within his trousers. It demanded release to explore her tender flesh.

Sheathing his claws, he dipped a finger into her wetness and slid it along her inner walls. When she moved with him, he pulled the digit out. He ran it lengthwise along her slit. She thrust against him on the downstroke and his finger slipped to her anus.

She stilled.

"Ah-ha. No one has fucked you here yet."

She shook her head.

Slowly, he lifted his finger to her wet core and dipped in, coating the digit well. He pulled his finger out and moved lower to her dark hole.

He circled the rosebud with teasing strokes. He knew how sensitive the flesh around the center was. Laurel widened her legs granting him access to her forbidden treasure, but he stopped and placed his arms on either side of her.

The look of need she gave him he would take to his grave.

He leaned forward covering her and pressing his trousers against her sensitive flesh.

A moan escaped her. He imagined the buttons of his trousers rubbed all along her, from clit to anus.

"Do you want me to fuck you?"

She looked at him, her brown eyes glossed with arousal. She nodded her acquiescence.

"Answer with words my heart." He kissed the sensitive column of her neck.

She shook her head.

"What my heart?" He enjoyed the various shades of pink she turned. He smiled over her embarrassment at saying the crude word.

He moved to rise and those buttons must've sent such shivers along her flesh, for her next words burst from her mouth. "Yes. Fuck me."

She arched her hips against him.

He rose above her, "Patience, my heart." He reached for the first button on his trousers.

An amber fire glowed in her eyes and he sensed rebellion. Perhaps because he'd denied her desire. He sensed his wife was denied very little these days.

"Calm yourself, my dear. You mustn't have your way all the time, you'll be spoiled." He slowly unbuttoned.

She lifted her head to view his progress and apparently admired the results. She licked her lips.

"If you keep doing that I'm going to tup you straight away."

"Go ahead. Tup me. I don't mind. I'm not going anywhere." She smiled as she tossed his words back at him.

Once his cock was released he wasted no time and slid the length into her cunt, she gasped, and he retreated.

"Continue husband, your attention is a good thing." She pushed her hips forward taking in what she had lost.

He leaned down claiming her lips, crushing her hips to his. He lifted his head to lift a nipple to his lips and roll it between his teeth. He didn't protest when her fingers sought the buttons of his shirt.

She tugged frantically rather than taking care to salvage the tiny obstacles. Once her task was complete, her hands slipped inside to caress the length of his back.

It was hard to reconcile this passionate, demanding woman with the wife of his youth. The familiar touch of fingers along his spine reminded him of the woman of his past and what she meant to him.

Ben tried to slow his strokes and savor the moment wrapped in memories, but Laurel would have none of it.

Her hand slid beneath his trousers pushing the material further down his legs and moving her heels to press him further into her with every push. She continued to answer his thrusting hips with her own demands. She rose to meet his urgent thrusts rubbing against him.

Their dance was a primal rhythm their bodies remembered, even as their minds struggled to regain what was lost.

Ben felt the involuntary tremors of her second orgasm.

Laurel cried out with shameless abandon.

He rode the waves of her shattering release before finding his own.

CHAPTER SIXTEEN

*B*en collapsed backward toward the nearest chair, his shirt open and pants around his ankles.

"Well that was rather pleasurable," his wife said sitting up. Her corset remained on and her stocking-clad legs parted where he'd left her giving him a lovely view.

"I thought so too," he bent over to retrieve his pants.

"Are you leaving?"

"Do you want me to stay?"

"I thought you might. I meant what I said, you are welcome here. If you don't wish to stay with me, I can arrange for a separate room." She rose from the bed retrieving an ivory robe from her armoire.

"Are you sure?" Even though he'd tupped his wife, in many ways they were still strangers from their long years apart.

She walked over to where he sat. She bent at the knees, kissed him on the forehead, and tilted her head slightly to the side. Her brown eyes shined and her lips parted slightly before she spoke. "I love you. I want to be with you. I want you with me. What do I need to do to show you how much I want this?" Laurel gestured her hand between their bodies.

"I'll stay." Ben forced the words out through the swelling of emotion in his throat.

"Good." She walked over to the sideboard and pulled a cord off to the side of it. Within moments there was a knock on the door.

Laurel cracked it open.

"Yes, mum." Ben heard the voice of Libby, the maid.

"Could you bring a plate of dates and nuts for my guest?" Laurel leaned away from the door, turning her head. "Do you want any more food, husband?"

"Scotch."

"And some scotch please Libby."

"Certainly, mum." The door closed with a click.

"Well let us get you some bedclothes."

He watched her next movements in fascination. His wife lowered to her hands and knees. He much enjoyed watching her dive under the bed with her heart-shaped bottom waving like an invitation. Once she rose from her task, she would see his response since he had yet to put on his trousers.

"Ah-ha!" she wriggled further under the bed flattening herself against the floor.

"You're going to get dusty retrieving whatever you want under there," he said callously.

Her derriere disappeared from his view, despite him leaning over in the chair to maintain a better look.

"It will be worth it," her muffled reply came.

Ben leaned back in the chair, knowing by the tone in her voice she wouldn't be deterred.

He watched her rounded buttocks come back into view. She slid backward onto her knees with a leather satchel obviously retrieved from the furthest recesses under her obstacle of a bed.

Dust collected along her sleeves and sprinkled in her hair like moss on an old tree. Her triumphant smile produced a shine beneath the dirt. "I found it!" she declared.

"So, I see." Ben's mouth turned up with her enthusiasm.

Laurel stood, taking the satchel with her over to the empty sideboard and placing the bag on top. She rummaged through it, humming as she performed the task. At that moment, he saw his wife, the woman he married. She was beneath the surface, protected by circumstances and false bravado. He was enamored at having found her, and he quit paying attention. He wrapped himself in memories and his heart whirred with a sentiment he thought long dead.

"What do you think?" her question interrupted his musings.

Ben struggled to clear his mind of the fog. He looked up to find Laurel dangling a piece of material in his face. He fought to clear his vision.

She held out a smoking jacket, which she'd given him for their first Christmas. Even though he'd never worn one, she bought him one saying, 'You will be so dashing.'

"Hey, that's mine." Ben grabbed the silk wanting a piece of the past between his fingers.

"Yes, I have your clothes and supplies from when we were in Crimea. I sent Omar back to retrieve them from the Sultan," she answered.

Ben retrieved his trousers from his ankles and haphazardly buttoned them before walking over to the sideboard. Looking in the bag, he pulled the items out: two shirts, a nightshirt – which he never wore-- his French foreign legion uniform, a stethoscope, folding magnifying glass, and scalpel. Finally, he retrieved the silver pocket watch he received from his father's family in Scotland when he graduated from Edinburgh. Inside was a Gaelic saying, 'Nuair a thig air duine thig air uile.' Essentially meaning, 'When it comes on one it comes on all.' Ben wasn't sure what it meant, but he was glad to have the watch back again, nonetheless.

"Why did you keep these things?" he asked.

"They are yours, part of you." Laurel looked at the floor before continuing, "I used to sleep with your shirts and nightclothes, even the robe. Those items smelled like you and my happiest memories were with you. Your 'things' got me through the very worst days. It was as if I still had a part of you." Her voice cracked. She sat on the edge of the bed.

Ben grabbed the robe and closed the distance between them in a few short strides.

"My heart, do not fret. I'm pleased you have these things from my— our past." Ben embraced her, and she seemed to burrow into his skin to escape whatever pain was chasing her.

Ben lifted the robe to his nostrils and inhaled. The scent was no longer his. The perfumes all over the fabric were Laurel's. The scarlet fabric was pungent with her warmth and laced with floral undertones. "It smells like you now," he leaned towards her, lowering his voice.

"I hope they still fit?"

At his quizzical look, she continued. "Of course, you are still an excellent male specimen."

"What are you trying to say, my heart?" He smiled at her unbidden yet strangled compliment.

"You are more muscular than when you last wore these clothes."

Ben gave her a quick squeeze before releasing her. He pushed himself to stand. "Let's see shall we?" He shrugged out of his shirt and put on the crimson silk jacket. "Still fits."

"I guess they are meant to be worn over bedclothes which you've not owned since I've known you." The rest of her words were lost.

There was a knock at the door.

She left him and he felt emptiness. He'd managed to survive all this time without her, it seemed unlikely she would impact him so. And yet, it was much like the first time they met. She'd always embraced him, and though they'd never spoken of it, he suspected she might know about his inner beast. He admitted he was less fearful of hurting her. Age had given her wisdom, as well as strength of emotion and spirit.

Libby entered with a tray of food. One could hardly call such an abundance food. It was far more decadent. More than dates and nuts, there were cookies, caramels, truffles, and mulled wine. The maid placed the food on Laurel's tea table

"Mum, would you like me to touch up your hair?" Libby nodded to the dust gathering in Laurel's disarrayed curls and wayward pins.

Laurel opened her armoire and considered her appearance in the mirror. "I think my hair will survive. I'll have Doctor Gunn help brush it out. Thanks, Libby, that will be all." She shooed the housekeeper out, following her until the door clicked once more and they were alone.

"You seem as though you would fit right in with the lords and ladies of Britain. Bossing servants around, ordering sweet treats—"

"Don't finish your sentence, Ben. I may talk like the upper crust, but you and I both know I have nothing in common with those insensitive snobs. I apologize if I sound and remind you of them from time to time. I assure you it has nothing to do with my fondness for them as much as mimicking those so I blend in." She poured a snifter of scotch for him.

"Why would you need to blend in?" he asked.

She tensed, but quickly waved aside his question, handing him a scotch when he approached.

"So, what looks good to you?" she asked before popping a truffle in her mouth.

He envied the bit of chocolate, which she rolled her tongue around.

"You," he said without guile. It was a simple statement of desire.

She smiled at him. His clockwork heart skipped and he looked forward to the night to come.

* * *

BEFORE DAWN, Laurel awoke to an empty bed. She sighed. It was probably too much to hope that her husband might stay the night. Looking towards the ruby-velvet, tufted bench at the end of the bed, she noticed his clothes were still folded where Laurel insisted he place them before going to bed.

Was he sleepwalking? A quick glance and she noticed the door was ajar. Laurel was stunned he still wandered in his sleep after all this time. When they were first married Ben told her he walked in his sleep. They used to move furniture in front of their bedroom door to keep him from wandering the halls and perhaps injuring himself in a trip or fall.

Resigned to find him, because she wasn't sure he was safe in a house full of witches and fae, she shoved her arms through the sleeves of her robe and walked down the darkened corridor. She felt the fear of another like a beacon pulling her along. She followed it to the balcony over-looking the garden. She immediately noticed the door to Molly's room was open. Of all the witches to wander in on, Molly was the least safe. Her recent attack made her dangerous should she decide to attack Ben.

Laurel peered inside, there stood Ben naked as the day his mother bore him.

Molly, with a look of terror, had backed into a corner of her room and had drawn a knife on him.

"Molly" Laurel quickly moved in front of Ben, to lead him back to their bed.

Molly started yelling, "Get out! Get out!" She jumped on the bed and started stabbing the knife in the air at Laurel.

"Quit your screaming!" Laurel fumed. How dare Molly! After Laurel took her in. "Are you on Dover's powder?"

"Me! There's nothin' wrong with me. Look at him!" Molly pointed at Ben.

Laurel turned to face her husband. He was in a typical trance-like state, but she inhaled sharply when she noticed his usual bright forest green eyes were red.

"Laurel, your husband is the god-damned Cleaver!"

CHAPTER SEVENTEEN

Laurel couldn't believe her husband might be, 'The Cleaver of Constantinople' as the papers reported. Not Ben! Not the man who had saved many lives during the Crimean War. She simply couldn't imagine he would go against his very nature and kill.

Laurel looked at her husband. He seemed to still be in a hypnotic state. She turned her head and issued a command. "Molly, shush!"

Molly, ever the good soldier, quieted and moved closer to Laurel's back. "What's wrong with him?" she asked.

"He's sleepwalking. Did this the first few years we were married, too."

Molly pushed her left hand over Laurel's shoulder waving it in front of Ben's rigid face. "His eyes are open."

"Sometimes they open." She turned her head to speak to Molly.

"Why are his eyes red?" Molly pulled her hand back from between Laurel and Ben.

"I don't know. I'm not the doctor here. He is." Laurel tilted her head towards her husband.

"Cleaver has red eyes, he does." Molly retreated to the furthest corner of her bed.

Laurel sighed. "I know. I'm going to bring Ben back to my room and lock him in." Laurel was fortunate she had one of two rooms that could lock in The Horizontal. The other was Molly's.

Laurel ushered her husband out.

"I'll lock my door behind you." Molly rose from the bed and trailed them.

"No." She turned back to face her frightened friend. "Why don't you order some breaky and tea. I'll be back and we'll discuss the night of your attack as well as what has transpired here." Laurel had let Molly avoid the conversation long enough. Now she needed answers and she hoped it wouldn't be too late to save Ben.

* * *

AFTER LAUREL LEFT, Molly locked the door anyway. Laurel could damn well knock. She admitted to hunger. Her stomach growled. Daylight peeked through the windows casting light amongst the shadows, indicating others would be rising soon enough. She walked over to the golden cord behind the door and pulled.

A few minutes later a maid arrived. She was a young thing with dark eyes and hair. Looked a bit like Fatima without the curves.

"Yes, missy?" the doe-eyed girl asked.

"Can you bring some tea and breakfast?"

"Yes, missy."

"And let Libby know Lady Laurel will be joining me." She told the fawn before she retreated.

"Of course, missy."

Once the door clicked shut, Molly locked it again. She dressed. She hadn't for days, but now there was no reason not to. She chose an aqua and silver tartan plaid day dress to go over her emerald combat corset, linen bloomers, and dark stockings. A velvet jacket, the color of dark pine, with a matching top hat finished her ensemble. She was about to don the jacket when there was a knock at the door. She opened it to find Laurel dressed and ready.

"I've ordered breakfast and tea, "she said, extending her arm.

"You locked the door." Laurel wore a periwinkle walking jacket and skirt. There was Venetian point lace at the hem of the skirt matching the cuffs of her jacket. Glass beads strung above the lace along the hem matched the buttons on Laurel's ivory linen blouse. She infiltrated the room to sit on a rough-hewn chair next to a bare table, before smoothing her cotton skirt.

Molly's furniture may not be as modern as the rooms in the main house, but she had acquired the pieces on her own. The Persian carpet she'd purchased in the marketplace. The bedding of linen and silk was given to her by a generous lord.

"Do you blame me?" Molly closed the door, latching it shut.

"No. I suppose not, but Molly, if you had told me about the ghosts, Dover's powder, or even the night of your attack, I could've perhaps protected you. Instead, you didn't trust me, let me give you the boot, and hid behind my skirts rather than speak with the authorities."

"I've spoken with Inspector Clarke." Molly lifted her chin.

"When?" A glimmer of panic crossed Laurel's features.

"Last night. I haven't had a chance to tell Raven your dear spouse is The Cleaver, but I will." Molly would not be intimidated into keeping her silence, not about this, and not by Laurel.

"You don't know anything, Molly. Ben is not The Cleaver."

"Just because you don't want him to be a killer does nae make it true. I personally don't know what I'd do if a man in my bed was a cold-hearted killer."

"Let me talk to Ben before you go running to Inspector Clarke." Laurel touched Molly's arm.

"Why? So the two of you can come up with an alibi."

"No. I need to know for myself." Laurel's eyes glistened with moisture.

Molly would not feel guilty about this. She'd barely escaped the madman, and she had no intention of living under the same roof with him.

There came a knock at the door. Molly rushed to answer it. Libby was there with a tray. Molly extended the door and Libby placed the tray down on the empty table. "Are you alright Mum?" she asked Laurel.

"I'm fine Libby. Thank you for bringing breakfast." Laurel smiled at the servant, dismissing her with a wave of her hand. She was sorely mistaken if she believed Molly could be dismissed as easily.

"Laurel - we are not safe with your husband in residence." Molly pleaded with Laurel to see reason.

"I'm telling you, Molly, he can't be The Cleaver."

"Why?"

"He simply can't!" Laurel placed her hands on her hips. "Do you know what it means to me to have found him?"

"I--"

"It's like the other half of my soul has returned. I know you're scared, but I'll not let you or anyone else take him away from me." Laurel stared pointedly at her.

"What about your safety? Who will see you remain unharmed?"

"I will. I've already locked him in my room. I'll continue to lock him in with me each night so everyone is safe."

Molly's brows drew together and her face tightened.

"You are not the only one among us with gifts." Laurel lifted her chin.

"You've never revealed any gifts." How did Laurel keep such secrets? Molly had been as close to her as anyone.

"Well, not gifts exactly. Power might be a better word. I'm not like you." Laurel answered, turning away.

Was it possible? Could Laurel be Fae? Molly wondered if Laurel was baiting her. The brotherhood had assigned her to Laurel. Did they know? She should have suspected Queen Morgan wouldn't want Molly to spy on a mere witch.

"I'll ask Moody to stay with us. If anyone knows anything about Ben's condition it will be him."

Molly kept her distance and ignored the knot in her stomach.

"Victoria sent word your recital will be the entertainment at Commodore Emory Pembroke's upcoming ball."

"Since when does the Commodore host balls?" Molly was fine with the change of subject.

"I'm not sure, but we will have to get you ready."

"The man is such a stuffed peacock."

"True. This ball did make me think of your other skill set."

"My music - yes. I will have to find a piece to resonate with the people." A sensation of relief came over her and Molly's spirits lifted. Music would soothe these times of trouble.

"I was thinking about your skills as a seamstress. You've got obvious talent." Laurel gestured at Molly's ensemble. "Perhaps you'd like to become The Horizontal's resident seamstress. You wouldn't have to entertain either with music or otherwise."

Molly recalled the dreams she and her sister Emma had of owning a shop together before they were separated and each recruited by the Brotherhood. "I will think about it." Molly's voice lost its power.

"Very well. I suppose I must see which girls are invited to attend the ball." Laurel left without touching her breakfast and Molly couldn't bring herself to eat.

Molly left the room to search for Inspector Raven.

CHAPTER EIGHTEEN

*L*aurel stopped Omar on her way back to her room and asked him to send word to Moody at Ben's flat.

She didn't look forward to the conversation with her husband and approached her room cautiously. She turned the key slowly hoping he was still abed.

"You locked me in?" The question greeted her and she flinched.

"I had no choice. You were sleepwalking."

The color drained from his face.

"Here, sit down. I'll order you some coffee."

"No." His jaw tightened and his eyes narrowed. "Tell me what happened."

"At some point in the night, you must've awakened and walked. You went all the way to the courtyard. I found you in Molly's room," she answered, turning her face away from him.

"Did I hurt her?" Ben paced the room like a caged animal.

"No."

He avoided her eyes and clenched his fists.

"You merely scared her." Laurel smoothed her hands on her skirts.

"What are you not telling me?" Ben looked pointedly at her hands.

"Please sit down." She reached out and touched her fingers to his bare arm, leading him to the nearest chair.

Once he settled, she sat across from him. Laurel wished she had eaten. Hunger caused her stomach to turn.

Ben inhaled.

It reminded her of the calming breaths he had done before surgery. He had told her it helped him steady his hands before working on his patients.

She took a deep breath of her own before she spoke. "When I found you, Molly was in the corner of her room terrified."

Ben's green eyes opened wide. "You said I didn't hurt her."

"You didn't, but she was scared of what she saw in your eyes." Laurel reached her hand across the table.

He crossed his arms over his chest. "Spit it out, Laurel."

"Your eyes were red." She pulled back resting her hands on her lap.

"Bloodshot," he corrected.

"No. The iris and pupil were red, like blood."

"That's impossible," he protested, raising arched eyebrows.

"Is it? You are not the same man I knew. You have changed. I'm not even sure how you sit before me when I watched you die." The idea Ben might be The Cleaver tore at her insides.

"I have a clockwork heart, put there by the best physicians."

"At what cost?" Apprehension coursed through her.

"What are you saying?"

"Ben, you arrived here, now. The Cleaver has killed near my establishment and those closest to me. Molly believes you are The Cleaver and I'm not sure she's wrong. I want her to be, but how can I be sure?"

"I would never hurt you." He reached for her.

She shook her head and leaned further into her chair. "You've never known what you do when you sleepwalk. Are you still blacking out? Do you remember anything?" Questions poured from her like a runaway train.

"I have no memory." His expression was a facade of stone.

"Is it possible you are a monster?" She pressed him, wondering if he knew what he was and if she could truly control him.

"I don't know." Ben hung his head.

"Perhaps it's for the best if you stay here and I can lock us in every night."

His green eyes became flat and as unreadable as stone. "What if you are my next victim?"

"I've asked Moody to come. He will ensure no harm comes to either of us." At his look of befuddlement, she continued. "Don't worry. He won't sleep with us as he did when he was a child. I'll have him settled in the blue room, down the hall."

"Moody? Are you sure you want the boy involved in this?"

"Boy? Ben please, Moody is a man full grown and more than capable of taking care of you. You've watched him grow into adulthood, likely seen him come into his powers." The loss of those years was too painful for her to recall. What did she want from him? She longed for peace of mind. He was still her husband, and now worried she may have lost her dreams of leaving this place. Could she go on by herself? She believed so, but why should she have to when he was here?

"I'm sorry." He couldn't seem to bring himself to look at her.

Laurel needed to think and without looking back she left.

* * *

BEN MANAGED to get himself dressed in yesterday's suit by the time Moody showed himself in.

"I see Mu— Laurel moved you into her apartments." Moody wore his usual black suit like a uniform. It was no wonder people often mistook him for a servant.

"For now. I understand she will have you down the hall." Ben confirmed.

"Omar explained the situation to me." Moody walked around the room, lifting small objects. "Has she shown you the jeweled heart?"

"No. And as you know, you are here for other reasons."

"You were sleepwalking. What did you do to cause her concern?" Moody asked.

"It seems I scared The Cleaver's latest victim, Miss Molly Flannigan. Apparently, my eyes resemble The Cleaver's."

"Oh? He has green eyes?" Moody gave him a knowing look.

"He has red eyes like blood," Ben stressed with a grim twist to his mouth.

"And your eyes were red when you were sleepwalking?" Moody appeared to contemplate the question.

"Apparently."

"Any other unusual features?" Moody asked.

"I didn't sprout horns or wings if that's what you're getting at." Ben was unsure why he expressed a specific image.

"Any out-of-place memories?"

"No. It's like every other time I've blacked out. Nothing is there. Perhaps I've done terrible things."

"No, sir. You've done nothing wrong. I'm certain of this." Moody spoke with such conviction Ben almost believed him. "I will check on Miss Molly and ensure she is safe and hale."

* * *

ONCE MOLLY WAS DRESSED she moved with all haste to the lower levels to find Inspector Raven.

She rapped loudly on his door. Her hand stung and turned pink along the knuckles. The door swung open. She jumped back. Dominique Augustine stood before her. Molly was undeterred. "I'm looking for Inspector Raven."

Dominique widened the door to allow Molly entrance. Raven stood in the background lazily putting on a milky white shirt that matched the rustled sheets. "I can send him to your room once he is dressed." The woman seemed to mock Molly with her American drawl.

"Yes." Molly turned on her heel and fled to her room. Even if Raven followed her, he would not catch up. Once inside, she shut the door and paced the room. She finished her third lap when there was a knock on the door.

Without hesitation, she pulled on the handle. "You needn't rush here on my account –" she forgot the rest of her witty sentence as a stranger stood before her.

The man had dark skin and short raven-colored hair threatening to curl if it grew any longer. He wore a black wool suit with a cream-colored linen shirt. He was young. She guessed he'd walked the earth less than two decades.

"Hello, Miss Flannigan. We haven't had the pleasure to meet. I'm Moody Jinn."

Molly stared into his golden eyes and saw the inferno ready to consume her. "Demon, get out! You cannot enter here." She looked for a cross and found naught. She chastised herself for not being pious. Molly made the motion of crossing herself, hoping to protect herself from such evil.

"I'm not a demon. Although my mother was likened to one many times," his silky voice teased her.

Molly watched helplessly.

He crossed the threshold.

"Doctor Gunn wanted me to check on you. He is very concerned about your injury. I understood the doctor quite terrified you." Moody walked to her small table where breakfast sat getting cold.

"You won't erase my memories, you dream thief." Molly circled back and retreated towards the door.

"Would you like me to warm this for you?" Moody lifted the teapot and his hands glowed a bright orange beneath the skin, warming the metal kettle until it whistled. "There. Nice and hot for you." He turned back towards her. His obsidian eyes were like flames.

Molly's cheeks burned. The cut where The Cleaver struck felt like it was on fire. Molly clutched her bandage and turned to escape through the door, falling right into Raven's arms.

"Molly what's wrong?" he asked.

"He's a...he's a demon." She pointed back to where Moody stood by her small table. There was nothing but a gray swirl of smoke in his place.

"Who, Molly?" His brow furrowed. He looked to where she indicated.

"Doctor Gunn sent him. He said his name was Moody Jinn."

"Moody Jinn is a demon?" Raven frowned and his jaw tightened. He stood before her barely dressed. He wore wool trousers and his signature black boots, yet the shirt she'd seen him put on was barely buttoned revealing a patch of skin and a hint of dark hair on his chest.

"Yes. He works for Doctor Gunn, who has red eyes and is The Cleaver and sent Moody to steal my memories," the words tumbled from her mouth.

"Okay, Molly take a deep breath, and start at the beginning." Raven wrapped his arms around her and stroked her back.

She told him how she woke to find Doctor Gunn staring at her like a life-like automaton with blood-red eyes. How Laurel asked her to keep Doctor Gunn's attack a secret. Finally how they sent Moody Jinn to erase her memories. However, she didn't mention any of her suspicions about Laurel being Fae

"Why do you suggest he was going to wipe your memories?"Raven rubbed her back in soothing up and down motions. He showed such concern for her safety.

"Djinn are known to be dream thieves." Unbidden emotions bubbled to the surface. She gulped hard, and hot tears slipped down her cheeks. It wasn't pretty, delicate, or lady-like. She sobbed from her soul. Molly wrapped her arms around his tall and strong frame, holding onto him like he held her salvation.

Several minutes passed before the weeping dissipated. She put a small respectable space between them but did not break free of his hold.

Raven lifted her chin. "Molly, it'll be alright. I'll find this killer and keep you safe."

"Thank you, Raven." Her voice faltered, but she believed him and the corners of her mouth lifted.

Raven bent his head and kissed her.

Why was he kissing her? Perhaps he hated a woman's tears.

Raven released her chin. "I'm sorry, I forgot about your face."

Molly backed away from him, running to the small mirror above her wooden nightstand. She quickly removed the bandage, to see what damage had been done and gasped at her image.

"What is it?" In less than four paces he was by her side.

Molly's jagged scar was nothing more than a thin strawberry-colored line as if she'd had an incident as a child. It looked cauterized. It wasn't in the crude way Molly had witnessed on others. This looked like someone had burned the flesh neatly together somehow stitching it with fire.

"Incredible. Is this Doctor Gunn's handiwork?" Raven asked, reaching out to touch her flesh.

"No." Molly pulled back. "Doctor Gunn has an excellent hand, and I expected a scar like this in my old age, but I think Moody did this."

Raven gave her a puzzled look.

"I think he fixed me with fire. I told you he was a demon." She turned to face him.

"If he wanted to harm you, why heal you?"

"He didn't do it nicely. Why do you think I was screaming like a banshee before colliding with you?" She rested a hand on his chest.

Raven nodded. " I thought the doctor was a good man and I can't believe I misjudged him. I will solve this mystery, Molly. No matter where the truth leads."

CHAPTER NINETEEN

*L*aurel was relieved to be reunited with her husband. Though with this Cleaver business was proving problematic and her decision to extract herself from British control was easier said than done. While the world saw her as obligated to Queen Victoria until the Persian Empire chose either to remain neutral or side with Britain. If it were only so simple. Although the queen wouldn't be satisfied until she had a foothold in Constantinople, Victoria was still unlikely to release her, due to Laurel's Fae status. Laurel was considered the property of the crown given to the royal family by her own father, Daniel Kavanaugh, in exchange for title and lands.

While Ben left with Moody to retrieve some of their belongings in the flat, Laurel made her way to the courtyard. She sought out Aaron where he kept a room. He'd always offered her good counsel before when it came to British political scandals. At least he could offer a human perspective.

The sun was in its late afternoon zenith and some of the girls were enjoying tea and crumpets informally on the lower level in the courtyard. She continued along the cobblestone walkway until she'd reached the outside of his room. She paused as she heard the tell-tale signs of love-making on the other side.

She walked to the center of the courtyard and visited with Dominique as well as the new girl from Nippon. Libby and a few others had gathered to enjoy a cool beverage in the center of the courtyard. "What are you ladies enjoying this afternoon?"

"I'm not sure you will approve, Madam," Dominique said, pulling the glass pitcher of dark liquid with floating ice towards her.

"Why is that? Is it some sort of contraband?" Laurel truly did not care if they violated the local liquor laws, as her own bar was stocked with alcohol from around the globe.

"I give you sweet tea, a beverage from the southern United States."

"Why must you Yanks take a perfectly good hot beverage and insist it be cold?"

Dominique poured and offered her a glass, "Why don't you try some?"

Laurel took the glass and tentatively took a sip. "It is sweet." She wondered how the Americans could stand such sickly sweetness. The concoction made her teeth ache.

"We made a few modifications. Typically, we pour on loaf sugar back home. I used honey in this recipe. You have it more readily available, but I don't think it tastes quite as sweet."

When Dominique finished explaining the finer points of her recipe, the door to Aaron's room opened. Laurel had expected to see Molly emerge, but Lieutenant March had been hosting Anastasia, one of the Russian girls.

Laurel didn't care who Aaron slept with. She never had. They both had their assignments and were required to achieve their objectives by any means necessary. However, Laurel knew Molly held sentiments for Aaron and worried at the Irish witch's reaction upon Aaron's conquests parading from his room.

Laurel looked over her shoulder to the balcony and was relieved Molly's room was shut and she was nowhere to be seen. She shook off her concern and continued to Aaron's room. When she tapped on the door, he replied, "Come in."

She opened the door to find him strapping his arm on.

Aaron turned to look at her. He pulled the strap tight using his teeth, his lips lifted in a half-smile. He finished looping the leather through the buckle with his hand before asking, "What is botherin' you, Lovey?"

"I see you are spreading your affections around," she said with a stitch of discontent.

"Don't be that way. You know things have changed now since your husband has returned."

"I do," she conceded. "My husband is what I came to speak to you about."

"Do tell." His eyebrows furrowed.

"I want him, Aaron. I've only ever wanted him," she confessed.

"So be with him," he sighed.

"I don't want to run the queen's brothel. I've always wanted to settle down. It was the whole reason I married. I realize the irony of marrying an American in the French Foreign Legion." A wry glint appeared in his eyes, and his expression remained stoic.

"I see. You want out of the contract with the queen." He seemed to have an uncanny ability to figure her out. If not for the vision of his death by fire, she would not have thought him human.

"Yes."

"Afraid there is nothing you can do, Lovey. You are well and truly ensnared."His words dashed the last of her hope.

"Truly?"

"Not without being tried for treason."

"I've done nothing treasonous!" Despite her status, she would never betray England. "I've gathered all sorts of nasty little secrets for the government of Britain. I never once received a thank you or asked for anything. " Not even her freedom.

"Betrayal is irrelevant. It's the secrets you know which make you dangerous. Of course, there is also the value of future secrets you might uncover. However much the queen may like you personally, she cannot and will not let you out of your obligation."

Laurel walked and sat on the end of the bed, she folded her hands almost in prayer. "Are you absolutely certain?"

"I am." He sat next to her. "We could ask Commodore Pembrooke. The man has never been a fan of your establishment, despite the useful information gained on the Great Alliance. He holds more power now. Let us speak to him at his upcoming ball." He put his arm around her shoulder and squeezed tight.

"Yes, that would be wonderful. Thank you, Aaron." Laurel couldn't resist and returned his embrace.

"Well, aren't you a fickle woman, Mrs. Gunn?" Inspector Raven Clarke's voice rang from the doorway, which Laurel had left open.

Laurel detached herself from Aaron to face her accuser. "There is nothing improper going on here Inspector." She stood placing her hands on her hips. "What do you want?"

"Molly came to speak to me about your husband's attack on her last night as well as Mr. Jinn's attack this morning."

"What accusations has Molly brought forth?" Laurel crossed the room until her skirt touched Raven's boots.

"Is Molly okay?" Aaron asked behind her.

"She is fine." Laurel waved him off with her hand. "Inspector, I'm not sure what Molly told you, but I can assure you she is exaggerating. My husband was sleepwalking and it gave her quite a fright when she awoke. As for Moody, he wouldn't harm anyone." Laurel spoke with a conviction she felt in her bones. She had not raised the boy, yet, she did not believe he would harm the innocent, despite his power.

"Are you certain? I understand he can create fire in his hands."

"Can he now?" So, Moody had fully matured. Laurel knew when she purchased him at the slave market he was special and would have some wonderful abilities. The seller told her to never remove the iron collar from his neck, and the boy would remain her property, loyal only to her. The minute they left the marketplace she sought out a smithy and had the unsightly band cut off.

"When he displayed his power he had red eyes like The Cleaver, as does your husband." Raven leaned forward to intimidate her.

"Well, I'm sure my husband has taught him many tricks from the circus." How dare the inspector bring accusations up in front of Aaron. Was he trying to stir up trouble or was he ignorant?

"Which is it, Mr. Clarke, her husband or this Moody? You can't have both being The Cleaver." Aaron muscled his way between Laurel and Raven.

Laurel was relieved he hadn't grasped onto the paranormal elements in Inspector Raven's story.

"That's Inspector," Raven said before leaning sideways. "What is your relationship with Mr. Jinn?" He asked Laurel, raising his voice.

"If you must know, Moody is my adoptive son. Surely, you know this is not the time or place for such questions." Laurel moved to stand at Aaron's side.

"Madam, what I know is you are surrounding yourself with suspicion by not revealing everything to me. I cannot help you if you do not help me. I will not find The Cleaver before he kills again if you do not share information with me."

"Not all information is relevant to your case, Mr. Clarke. Are we not allowed some measure of privacy?" Aaron asked.

"Inspector, not Mister. I won't tell you again, Lieutenant."

"You don't need to. These are my private quarters, and I'm commanding you to leave."

Raven said not another word before he left.

Aaron turned to face her. "Lovey, what have you gotten yourself into?"

"Nothing. My husband has returned from the grave, Moody is my beloved son and apparently one or both are The Cleaver." She said sarcastically and waved her hand in dismissal.

Aaron opened his arms and she went willingly to them. She desperately needed to have someone on her side and if her former lover was willing to stand as her friend she dared not deny his support. She was desperate.

* * *

BY THE TIME Moody and Ben arrived back at The Horizontal, evening had fallen. Ben found Laurel in her sitting room where they'd last spoken.

She seemed sad. "What's wrong, my heart?" He immediately went to her side.

"Molly went to Inspector Raven this afternoon." She stared down at her lap.

"So, he knows." Ben suspected he might have lost an ally.

"He knows. Moody went to Molly's room and performed magic."

"Moody told me." There was no sense in denying it. He would have to navigate these waters and decide the best course of action.

"Did he say why?"

"He told me he wanted to help." Ben didn't need to give further details about Moody's magic, though he suspected she might know.

"Well, he succeeded in casting doubt on himself as well." Laurel continued, "In Raven's mind you are both strong suspects as The Cleaver."

"Laurel." He walked over to her and knelt before her, pressing into her skirt. "I can assure you Moody is most assuredly not The Cleaver."

"What about you?" She raised her face. Her dark brown eyes met his and he could see the concern, fear, and doubt within their depths.

133

"I wish I could be as certain. I've been experiencing blackouts and sleepwalking. I'm not sure what I'm capable of in those moments." He held nothing back, knowing if he did, he put her at risk. Once he bared his soul about his lost time and his concern he might be The Cleaver, she could walk away from him. It would leave him broken, but she would be safe. At the end of the day, Laurel mattered more to him than his contentment.

"I can't believe you would ever harm anyone intentionally. Certainly not me, I feel it in my heart." She pressed her fingers to the middle of her chest.

He smiled, watching her fingers tap her sternum. "You have no idea how much I want to believe I'm not some monster."

"We'll navigate this like we always have. From the day you proposed and I went against the wishes of my father to marry you, we've overcome many obstacles including your death. This is no different. We must continue this honesty between us. It will help to find the truth. Once the truth is known we will move forward."

Ben couldn't resist. He kissed his wife. She was stronger than he gave her credit for. He loved her unrefined blunt speech. The only other time her polished exterior disappeared was when he made love to her. She was a wild thing possessed. Her passion rivaled his own. He was desperate to have her there.

She responded to his kiss as he hoped, crushing her lips against his. Her cries got lost in his mouth.

Laurel pushed him towards her bedroom stripping his jacket and fumbling with his shirt buttons.

"Stop." He held his ground.

She gave him a bewildered look.

"Let us both remove our clothes. There's no reason we need to have items mended due to our uncontrollable passions." He smiled.

"Agreed," she replied.

He removed his jacket, setting it on the rocker in her room. "Are you going to remove your clothes?"

"I thought I might enjoy the show." She moved to lift his jacket off the rocker and placed it on the coat rack in the corner.

"Are you going to hang all my belongings?"

"No. Ironing is much easier than mending." There was a faint glint of mischief in her eyes.

"Fine." He removed his shoes before unbuttoning his shirt, watching Laurel's eyes as they brightened with pleasure.

She licked her lips.

He shrugged the sleeves free. His trousers were tight. Desperate to remove them, he slid them past his knees and shook them off with his socks posthaste.

His manhood jutted in front of him, and Laurel beckoned him to her. The invitation was a passionate challenge, hard to resist.

She leaned forward on the rocker and darted her tongue out to lick the moisture at the tip.

He arched his hips until her warm mouth closed around him. He released a groan at the eager strokes of her tongue tracing the fullness of his shaft.

Raising her head and tongue along his length, she gazed into his eyes.

"Enough!" He pulled her off him, lest he released before her. He dragged her up the length of him, the cotton and velvet of her clothes rasping along his now sensitive skin.

He kissed her with hungry persuasion, which belied his stoic words, "I believe you can leave your garments in a puddle too."

Laurel gave him a smile of power, knowing she had ensnared him.

His lips recaptured hers, more demanding this time. "Strip," he muttered, before setting her away from him.

Laurel did as bid, stripping away her cotton blouse with agonizing slowness on each button. She revealed the soft skin beneath. Unlike his clothes, hers were laid on the chair with care. She remained facing away from him. She undid the buttons on her heavy skirt, letting it pool around her feet. Her bloomer-covered derriere offered to his manhood.

"Remove your drawers," he commanded.

Once the offending garment was removed, she turned and stood before him wearing her chemise, stockings, and boots.

Ben sat on the edge of her bed. "Come here."

She stood between his legs and he reached down to touch her womanhood, barely covered by the fabric of the chemise. She was hot and wet, ready for him.

Pulling his fingers to his mouth he licked them, reveling in her taste.

Ben removed the chemise pulling the fabric over her head. He nuzzled her bare breasts, inhaling her scent. He lifted the globes in his hands, rubbing the pads of his thumbs across her nipples. He reclaimed her mouth, crushing his lips to hers.

Ben pinched her nipples and she whimpered. He moved her hands to her back and pulled her with him to the bed and she was sprawled atop him.

"Ride me, wife," he suggested.

A light illuminated her eyes. She took him in hand and guided his erection to her velvet warmth. She was intoxicating. Laurel set the pace, riding in torturously slow movements.

He bucked and arched beneath her.

When she dipped low, he captured her breast in his hand and ravaged the nipple with his tongue and teeth.

She arched into his assault. Her breath came in short, harsh gasps. Her hot sensuality brought him closer to his peak. If she didn't climax soon, he would beat her to it.

Ben was on the ragged edge. He thought he would expire when she convulsed around him in glorious waves of splendor and he found his release.

As her limbs clung to him, he kissed her, "I love you."

* * *

IN THE AFTERMATH of their love, Ben curled on his side and fell asleep. Laurel looked at his feet peeking out beneath the covers. His feet looked rather monstrous. His nails seemed to grow at a rapid rate. Her husband always trimmed the nails on his hands daily, if not a few times a day. His feet, however, he'd let go. They were covered most of the time. The nails would get long enough they resembled claws. He could also curl his toes forward around a pipe, bed frame, or even the back of a strong chair. It was akin to a bird on a perch. It had served Ben well in the circus when he performed acrobatic stunts like trapezing, tightrope walking, and leaping through rings of fire.

His feet were not as strange as the half-moon scars running over his shoulder blades. According to Ben, his father possessed similar marks, and Ben believed they were a genetic anomaly. Laurel only wished she knew what fae possessed these traits. She lovingly ran her fingers across the scars and they seemed to move back pressing against her fingers.

Laurel quickly withdrew her hand and wondered if she imagined it or if perhaps Ben's breathing simply created the sensation.

CHAPTER TWENTY

Promptly at eight, the carriages arrived at the house to retrieve Dominique Augustine and Molly Flannigan. Laurel had managed to avoid Molly the past few days since she filed an informal report with the Inspector.

Laurel waited in her parlor watching for the girls to come down the stairs.

Dominique was the first to descend the stairs. She wore a gold gown with ruffled cap sleeves matching the ruffled bustle skirt. The bodice molded to her like a second skin, on her back was an embroidered gold and sky-blue orchid. A sky-blue sash trailed over the bustle errantly as though it was left untied. She wore her golden hair back in a bun at her nape.

Count Pierre Jean Claude stepped forward to help Dominique descend the last few steps holding her hand in his. "Mon chéri, you look stunning. You will be the gem of the ball."

Laurel agreed.

The couple retreated out the door.

Seamus O'Grady stood pacing The Horizontal lobby.

Laurel rose from her chair near the doorway and walked towards him. "Careful Seamus, you will wear a hole in my lovely Persian carpet."

O'Grady stopped. "Where is Mo—Miss Flannigan?" He crossed his arms in front of him and leaned back. He may have thought the stance puffed him up, but it merely pronounced his large stomach.

"I'm sure she will be down shortly," she responded. "You must practice patience, much like in politics." Nothing could be further from the truth. Ambassador O'Grady was known for pressing delicate issues at the Embassy. Aaron told her the man believed his was the only opinion to count, and would commonly interrupt the other speakers. Particularly those who sided with England. Aaron believed the man was a dissident. Laurel long suspected Molly fed information on O'Grady to Aaron.

Before Seamus could speak again, Molly made her way down the stairs. She wore a moss green dress with a matching sheer overlay. There were embroidered flowers in peach and gold along the hem and bodice of the dress and a three-tiered bustle on the back of the dress, adding to Molly's assets.

"It is about time." O'Grady's voice was sharp.

Laurel would've reprimanded him if she too didn't want to see Molly gone. She simply wasn't ready to speak with her yet.

She grimaced and bit her lip.

Seamus hauled Molly out the front door to his waiting carriage.

As those were the only two girls traveling by carriage, Laurel readied herself to go. She sent Ben ahead to ensure her girls left okay and The Horizontal was ready. There would be patrons in attendance following the ball and she wanted to ensure her bar was well stocked and girls were prepared for a rush in the early morning hours.

Laurel was ready to leave when Moody walked into the lobby.

"Mother," he nodded towards her and she took a step back. She was not prepared for the man he had become. He stood taller than her. His limbs were no longer gangly and it looked as though muscles bulged beneath his midnight black coat. Tears welled in her eyes. She had missed much.

"Moody, come here." She held her arms out to him. "I must hold you," her voice cracked.

He crossed the distance and though he didn't readily embrace her, she did him. "You, my child, have grown." Warmth emanated from him when he finally relented and his arms closed around her shoulders. She leaned back looking closely at the clear-cut lines of his profile. "Where is the boy I knew who could barely stay clean?"

"Ben insists on cleanliness." It was more of a statement.

Laurel released him and stood back. "I imagine he does. It is after all necessary in his profession. I see those fingers are still covered in ink." She nodded towards his hands.

"Yes." Moody shoved his hands into his trouser pockets.

"I am relieved you are staying here." She resisted the urge to embrace him once more.

"I live to serve." He shuffled on his feet.

"What does that mean?" She frowned at him.

"Nothing." He refused to meet her inquiring gaze and his body was rigid.

"What is wrong? We've never kept secrets, or at least we never used to." Her stomach clenched and she felt a tightness in her chest.

"I'm sorry," his voice cracked, making him sound younger. "I can't resolve our time apart."

"Moody, what are you playing at? You sent me away, remember?" Laurel could hardly forget.

"I do and I wish I never had, but I wanted you safe in the event I was unsuccessful"

Knowledge dawned on her. "You saved Ben? Are you the reason he is still among us?" she asked.

"No, that was Father. He went into a dormant state."

"A dormant...Wait. Do you know what kind of creature Ben is?" she asked wondering idly what had happened to Ben and Moody since.

"Miss," Omar called looking past Laurel. "Your Jumbo is ready."

"Thank you, Omar," she spoke over her shoulder

The door closed with a click.

She turned back.

Moody was gone.

Laurel quickly grabbed her wrap by the table and walked to the door where Omar had entered. Her ride to the Embassy was uneventful and quiet. It was exactly the rest she needed before entering the bustling building with a long night ahead.

Moonlight filtered through the windows above each column arch. Lamps lit behind each arch created a soft glow. Laurel found Ben emerging from a corner alcove. The soft lamplight danced against the hard planes of his face. He looked dapper in his midnight dress coat and matching trousers. He wore an obsidian black and silver tapestry vest. From his pocket hung the chain to the silver watch she had returned. Ben reached her side in minutes.

"Lady Gunn, you look delectable in that dress. The blue of cotton candy makes me want to eat you up." He wrapped his arms around her waist and whispered hotly against her ear.

She had dressed for him wearing an aquamarine gauze bodice and skirt with a royal blue sequined sleeveless tunic with gold embroidery matching the hem of the skirt. Below the hollow of her neck lay the heart-shaped jewel she received from the sultan. "Thank you, husband. Might I add you look dashing as well?"

"You may." He kept his hands on her waist. He escorted her to the long line of couples outside the main ballroom.

They waited with other couples until their names were called before entering the ballroom.

"Doctor Benjamin and Lady Laurel Gunn!"

Once inside Ben led Laurel to the Refreshment Room. Laid out on a long table were biscuits, cakes, cracker bonbons, and sandwiches. On either side were tea and coffee. In one corner, there was a man serving ices. She noted some younger girls from other establishments enjoying the selection of flavors. These girls seemed unattached and may have been brought in for the sole pleasure of the soldiers.

"Do you not want to dance?" she asked Ben. Though she detested socializing with politicians, she needed to plead her case to Commodore Pembrooke.

"I've not danced in ages, and certainly nothing as formal as a ball." There was a brooding gleam in the depths of his emerald eyes.

"I can show you." Laurel was happy to show him. She'd been trained from the cradle as her father always held hope she would marry above his station. Her kind were always meant to be bought and sold.

"Isn't the gentleman supposed to lead?"

"Have faith, husband. We will give the impression you lead in all things." Laurel reached for Ben's hand and led him to the dance floor. Once there they faced each other. "Okay my hand in yours and on your shoulder, and—"

Ben's hand immediately went to her waist, and his fingers splayed towards her buttocks. "I know where my hands go." He patted her bottom. He may know where his hands go, but he was choosing to break decorum.

"Are you trying to scandalize us?"

"Given your position in this town and the fact that we are married, I'm not sure how you could be further scandalized or why you are offended. If anything, observers will see you are a treasure belonging to me." He dropped his head towards hers.

There was a tingling in her stomach and she had to fight the overwhelming desire upon hearing his possessive claim. "No," she pulled back, "not here Ben."

He nodded, but the fire did not leave his eyes.

Laurel had to pull her gaze away from his and get back to the task at hand. She scanned the ballroom searching for Commodore Pembrooke.

Her husband wasn't as awkward as he would've had her believe. About halfway through the second song, he led her. Of course, he'd always been a quick study from her experience.

She made her way over to the punch bowl where Commodore Pembrooke stood with Miss Sophia Ostwald.

"Hello Commodore," she greeted Pembrooke and nodded, "Miss Ostwald."

"Mrs. Pembrooke." Sophia laced her arm through the Commodore's own.

Laurel clutched tighter to Ben's arm and leaned into him to prevent his fall. "Did you say, Misses?"

"Yes." Commodore Pembrooke answered, "Sophia and I were married this morning."

"And you still attended the ball?" The man must be made of stone, to not want the lovely Prussian in his bed immediately after marriage, or perhaps they had already consummated their union.

"Of course. A military man has no time for holidays. This event will serve just as well. We were announced upon our arrival, so everyone knows Sophia is mine." The Commodore seemed to puff up even more.

"Emory, you must not be so blunt with our guests." Sophia patted his captured arm with her other hand.

"Let Ben and I be among the first to congratulate you." What else could she say? She was in such a state of shock she was unsure whether the Commodore's marriage was to her benefit or demise.

Ben reached his hand out in congratulations and Commodore Pembrooke accepted.

"Will you be dancing this evening?" Laurel asked, hoping not to sound desperate.

"I'm a married man, Lady Gunn. I can't be caught cavorting with Constantinople's most popular courtesan." The Commodore huffed.

"Emory!" Sophia withdrew her arm from his.

Ben cleared his throat. It drew the Commodore's attention and kept Laurel from making a scene. "Commodore, I completely understand your concern in dancing with the city's most beautiful woman, my wife, so soon after nuptials with your beautiful bride. People would talk."

Laurel laced her fingers between his. He defended her with such ferocity, that she had a hard time believing he would harm her or anyone else.

"Harrumph." The Commodore wrinkled his nose and pressed his lips into a hard line, barely acknowledging Ben's speech.

"Thank you, Doctor Gunn." Sophia leaned forward, extending her hand toward him. Ben took Sophia's hand in his free one and lifted it to his lips.

"Congratulations my dear," he said.

Laurel leaned towards his ear, "I need to speak to Commodore Pembrooke about our future," she whispered.

"Lady Pembrooke, may I have this dance?" Ben bowed before Sophia and she accepted his hand. Laurel began her interrogation once Ben and Sophia were out of earshot.

"What do you want from me, Lady Gunn?" The question came out more as an order.

"Commodore, I know you are a busy man." She was a bit perturbed; he anticipated their conversation. She may have thought him fae if she had not seen his demise. Death by air.

"I am." He picked lint off his jacket.

"At Lieutenant March's suggestion, I would like to speak to you about the future of The Horizontal."

"Lady, I have no time for your establishment. If I had my way, The Horizontal would be as flat as your whores on their backs."

Laurel tried not to bristle at his course and wounding language. "We are of the same mind then, Sir. As I have recently reunited with my husband, my desire to peddle in the flesh trade has become unnecessary."

"So, close your doors." He made it sound so simple.

Laurel breathed in, praying for the patience of Job.

He continued his line of thought, "The moral standards have been lax far too long in the military. I'm a married man. I'd like to see my men follow my example. The Great Alliance is bothered by The Horizontal."

"Of course," she said. The Alliance was bothered by the queen's spies 'peddling flesh' to gain knowledge and weren't allowed to have a brothel. Only the English were allowed to procure a license from the Ottomans.

"I plan to raise a motion to clear the great city of all its sinful establishments, the opium dens, the public baths, and whore houses." He turned away from her as if to leave.

"That is a large undertaking sir." Aaron joined their conversation.

"And how do you feel, Lieutenant? You were in Lady Gunn's bed long before her husband arrived and as I understand it, many other beds," censure laced Commodore Pembrooke's voice.

"What I feel has no bearing. The lady is now married and if you choose to enforce the moral standards, I shall adhere to them. As it stands now, I shall continue to enjoy myself." Aaron smiled wide.

Laurel gave Aaron an incredulous stare. Would he risk irritating a commanding officer for his own pleasure? "How do you think the Prussians would vote if Commodore Pembrooke brought a moral measure forward?"

"I think they would be inclined to agree with such a law. They believe they have a higher moral code. The fact many frequent your establishment is of no consequence," his voice carried unique confidence.

"They don't frequent others?" she asked.

"Not as much as The Horizontal." Commodore Pembrooke grumbled.

"Surely, because I have the most beautiful, talented girls in the global city." Laurel couldn't help herself. She bragged and preened when it came to her establishment.

"Likely because you have the cleanest girls. No one has ever gotten the pox from your girls." Aaron corrected her.

Laurel felt herself deflating like a dirigible, after completing its trip. "What brings you here Lieutenant?" she snapped at him before she could temper her response.

"I came to escort you to the recital hall for Molly's performance." He offered her his arm.

"Of course." She rested her arm on Aaron's and let him lead her into the hall.

The opulence of the hall with its mullen pink walls and dome with gold details was like decadence on display. The light foam green added to the indulgence. Once Aaron stopped at her chair, Laurel sought out Ben but he was not there. Aaron sat next to her and Sophia nestled between Aaron and her husband.

"Where's Ben?" Laurel asked.

"I'm not certain. We got separated on the way here." She said demurely.

Where the hell was Ben?

* * *

IT HAD SEEMED simple enough to dance with her, allowing his wife to speak with Commodore Pembrooke. It felt more like an unsolvable puzzle.

"Have we met before Mrs. Pembrooke? You seem familiar to me." He asked before leading her in a waltz. Despite what he told Laurel he knew how to dance, and had learned at Edinburgh, but he was a bit rusty.

"I did not work for your wife as a whore, Doctor Gunn." She stiffened underneath his touch.

"I didn't presume you had. Perhaps you've attended Embassy functions before?" he asked.

"I have not." Her lips became a thin line.

"I didn't mean to offend. It is simply to ascertain why you look familiar." He smiled hoping to placate her.

She returned the smile, but it didn't touch her cool gray eyes.

They were quiet for several beats before she asked him. "How is Molly doing?"

It was his turn to stiffen. "She does well enough to perform this evening."

"She was fortunate the Cleaver sliced her cheek and not her carotid artery."

"That is an astute observation for a layperson." He nodded slowly.

"My father was a doctor," she sighed.

"Fascinating. Did you play nurse and assist him?" He tilted his head to the side. What an odd lady?

"Oh yes, He ran a hospital and it was my greatest pleasure to assist him in surgery and aid in the recovery of patients in his care." Her eyes shined and she stood a bit taller.

"Such a large undertaking for one so young. I would love to meet your father."

"He was killed." She swallowed hard.

"I'm sorry for your loss." He winced.

"No need to be sorry. He lives on in the patients he saved." Her sudden mournfulness dissipated like fog in the sun.

"What a wonderful point of view." Ben thought if he didn't love Laurel, this young lady would've made dents in his heart. "Perhaps I knew your father?"

"Do I understand you have a clockwork heart?" she asked.

"Yes." Did she perhaps hear it whirring in his chest?

"My father was one of the pioneers in creating clockwork mechanisms. He began with artificial limbs like Lieutenant March has, and graduated to organs including the gallbladder, spleen, kidney, and lung. He even created a mechanized eye. Yours is the first heart I've ever heard though."

"Is that so?" She'd piqued his curiosity.

"Most of the organs my father created were obsolete or they were duplicates, like the eyes and limbs. He'd been working on a liver before his death but had not yet perfected it. I'm certain the science behind your heart originated in his lab." She suddenly stopped and stepped back from him. It took Ben a moment to realize the music had stopped.

"Are you ready Doctor Gunn?"

A picture of a dark cold chamber with pitch-black iron bars, cold iron chains, and this woman flashed in his mind. The memory tore at his psyche, causing searing pain. He bent over, pressing his fingers to his temples, trying to will the throbbing and dark images away.

"Doctor, are you alright?" Sophia rested her hand on his shoulder.

"Get away from me!" He threw off her hand and backed away from her.

"So, you haven't forgotten me. You always were my favorite." She sneered and seemed to enjoy his struggle.

"Who are you?" He stared at her and more visions assaulted him. Moody in a cell with him. Screaming, blinding pain inflicted on him, on others.

"I'm Sophia, daughter of Doctor Ivan Ostwald, administrator of the Osiris Hospital. You were his greatest achievement. A clockwork heart.

We were never able to duplicate it and we tried many times. What makes you so special?" She reached her hand out to him again.

"Do not touch me!" It wasn't masculine, but he didn't care.

Doctor Benjamin Gunn turned and fled the hall to the alcove of the Embassy, exactly where he had met Laurel earlier. He was struggling to come to grips with the emotions towards Mrs. Sophia Pembrooke. He rested his hand against the iron gate, to steady himself.

The pain in his back wouldn't subside, something was bursting forth. Long leathery wings appeared at his side. His skull was next.

He felt the horns protrude from his head. This was the transformation he'd always wondered about. His skin took on an emerald hue.

Sophia's presence brought about his change. She was dangerous to him, Moody, and most of all Laurel.

Ben needed to find his wife. They must flee the global city. Events were moving too quickly for them to escape. Unfortunately, he couldn't move his feet. They were stone rooted to the floor. Ben watched in curiosity and horror as his limbs turned to stone.

CHAPTER TWENTY-ONE

Molly stood and took a central spot in front of the large ornate mirror trimmed in gold. The Prussian and Russian lords leered at her. She placed the Stradivarius beneath her chin.

It was hard to believe a few nights ago she had fought off The Cleaver.

Now she stood before an assembly of not only mighty and powerful men but also magical creatures of the fae.

A well-known pianist sat behind her, his attitude as pressed as his overly starched shirt. As a child of the theater, Molly missed performing for others. The theater hadn't provided enough opportunities for intelligence gathering for the brotherhood though.

She spared a glance towards Finn, who sat in the front row between Sophia Ostwald and Laurel. Absent was Doctor Gunn, which was fine with Molly as she took a deep breath and played Londonderry Air.

* * *

THE CLEAVER HUNG from a corner rafter. The footing was small, but he maintained his balance using a hook to hold himself steady. In his free hand, he held a crossbow. He would not allow Master's actions to dictate him. Molly Flannigan was a liability. No one survived him. No one. She would not be the first. He preferred to corner his prey where he had the element of surprise and could draw on their fear. Her survival pushed him to take risks. Risks that might reveal himself before others.

Molly Flannigan would not live to tell people what she remembered. He dared not take the risk she might put a face to her attacker.

He touched the tip of the arrow to one of the open lanterns lighting the hall. The fire on the arrow matched Molly's flaming auburn hair.

The bow was already cocked. All he had to do was release it. He waited until the violin reached the second stance. "Burn m'girl burn." He whispered before letting the arrow fly.

* * *

"It's The Cleaver," Sophia screamed and pointed to the rafters.

Laurel jumped and the villain hung on a hook before leaping to the ground below.

A flaming arrow flew towards Molly.

Victoria, who sat closest in the half circle, ran towards Molly. Possibly to throw her to the ground? Laurel couldn't be sure, as Victoria was shot in the back with a flaming arrow. Her alabaster embroidered tunic immediately caught fire.

Count Pierre Jean ran forward, throwing his cape across her back.

Laurel looked for Ben, but he hadn't returned. Raven had run off in immediate pursuit of The Cleaver.

Kage battled through the swarm of patrons to where his wife lay. He went down to her side.

Laurel did not think The Cleaver would attack Molly in public. It was foolish of her to try and re-launch Molly so close to her attack. Why? Why did she put others at risk to benefit her needs? Laurel lowered herself down to Victoria. The Count had already turned her over.

"Do you know what you are doing?" she sniped at him

"I was enlisted with one of the Foreign Legion's finest," he answered. He seemed to throw her irritation to the wind.

"Victoria, are you alright?" Laurel asked, assessing her friend from the front.

"She's unconscious, I think for the best. She should be moved to a more calm location. We must get her out of these clothes, though I fear some of the material may have burned to her delicate skin. Deep breaths Madame." Count Pierre spoke methodically, looking at Laurel.

Laurel agreed. "Omar!" She wasn't surprised to find her bodyguard right behind her.

"Ma'am."

"Commandeer Inspector Raven's carriage. He won't need it as he is in pursuit of the bastard who inflicted these injuries," Laurel commanded.

"Yes, Ma'am." Omar gave a curt nod and left her presence.

"Sir, this will not be comfortable for your wife. Pray she remains asleep," Pierre Jean spoke.

Kage moved to lift his wife.

Sophia approached. "Is there anything I can do? My father was a doctor."

"Mademoiselle, will you be so kind as to escort the ladies back to The Horizontal?" Pierre Jean nodded towards Dominique who watched in seeming horror as the events unfolded.

"Of course, Commodore Pembrooke lent me his carriage. I would be happy to escort Lady Gunn, Miss Dominique, and Miss Moll--" Sophie paused looking past Laurel to the small stage.

Laurel turned along with her stomach. "Molly!"

Where in the blasted hell was Molly?

* * *

STUPID MOLLY HAD RUSHED FORWARD to try and aid Victoria only for him to grab her about the waist and flung her into a grain sack.

In the fray, he knocked her against a wall and she must have blacked out.

Molly was awake now and no longer compliant. She resisted in earnest.

"Now, Molly quit struggling," The Cleaver hollered. He shook the burlap sack tossed over his left shoulder. He continued through the alleyway, along with the shadows until he reached the abandoned castle where he would meet his master.

"Oaf!" A booted foot managed to knock the wind out of him, and he stumbled.

"Enough of that now!" He shouted before dropping the bag and giving it a harsh kick.

A whimper from inside the bag satisfied him.

"Stay calm. We are almost there."

The sack remained still and silent.

"Thass a good girl then." He moved to pick up the bag when it moved.

The sackcloth rose like a creature of vengeance and stalked towards him.

He believed her stilled, yet in the moment of silence, it seemed Molly had gotten her bearings.

Now the bag lumbered towards him. What purpose she had, he didn't know.

His voice sank to croon, "Don't make me hurt you, Molly."

She continued bumbling forward towards his voice.

"All right then." The Cleaver readied his left fist.

When the burlap blob was within striking distance, he clocked her.

She fell to the left side of him, and he reached to pick her up, continuing towards his fate.

* * *

RAVEN ROUNDED the corner of the building, but he'd lost The Cleaver and Molly. The man was quicker than a human should be. He sniffed the air, but no scent was there. The creature smelled unhealthy.

He was making his way back through the main entrance when he caught Moody Jinn, also on his suspect list, standing in an alcove, staring at a statue very much resembling Doctor Benjamin Gunn, with two notable exceptions. It possessed large wings descending from his back and horns making him look like the devil.

"Mr. Jinn," Raven said.

"Inspector." The man spoke without taking his eyes off the statue.

"Have you seen Miss Molly?"

"No Inspector, I've rather been lost in thought." Moody motioned to the statue.

"Striking resemblance," Raven said.

"There is no resemblance. This is Doctor Gunn," Moody insisted.

"Are you certain?" If this was the case, Raven's prime and second suspect were both here.

"Oh yes. I was surprised it took him this long. Most gargoyles turn by the time they are a young adult."

"Did you say gargoyle?" Raven felt a tingle in his chest and sniffed at the statue, smelling nothing but stone.

"Yes. The creatures are born to guard places. Do you not have them in your land?"

"Not that I'm aware of. How do you know?" Raven edged closer to the statue.

"Well inspector, like you, I'm a bit of an investigator. Since I was a small child in Laurel and Ben's care, they made sure I didn't lack an education. I wasn't formally trained, but when we traveled, Laurel and Ben made sure I had access to libraries or tutors to advance my knowledge. When I grew older I was drawn more to the supernatural. I was curious about the origins of Doctor Gunn, especially following his death."

Raven heard the story of Ben's missing heart and let Moody continue.

"I discovered he was an abomination, much like me."

"How so?"

"Gargoyles are offspring of powerful fae. They are sterile and cannot produce offspring of their own."

"If they are truly fae children, there would be far more gargoyles and fewer monsters," Raven claimed.

"Sorry, I should have been clearer. Gargoyles are the offspring of the differing fae. Like a dragon and a mermaid. A wood sprite and a troll. Therefore, gargoyles all look different. They are the offspring of two powerful parents."

"What about werewolves and vampires?" Raven asked.

"They are genetically human, if they mate with a fae, they could likely have children who are magical like witches and warlocks, or another hybrid."

"Aren't gargoyles found on the sides of buildings?"

"Those are cursed with chains. Fae don't like dilution in their lines. They are rather purists. Young gargoyles, if caught, were chained with iron to a building and their hearts removed. The creatures turn to stone, a state of hibernation for them, and attach permanently. Sometimes the chained would guard the building against other supernatural beings."

"So, what prompted Doctor Gunn's change?"

"Fear and I think this iron gate aided in his acquiring this form."

Some gargoyles appear human and can remain in their living form to hide. I believe because Ben was never told what creature he was, he had not changed until now. And perhaps some never change. This may have been to protect him."

"So, you don't know what type of fae he is?"

"He is a being of fire as he has a tolerance for it, and he has dragon-like wings." Moody ran his hands along the wing confirming his opinion.

"How long will he be like this?"

"I don't know, but he can't stay here. I can't risk him being cursed to this place. I have a carriage outside. I'd like to get him back to his office."

"What about the gate?" Raven nodded towards Ben's hand.

"Easy enough." Moody shrugged.

Raven watched in fascination as fire emanated from Moody's hands and he cut through the iron like wax.

The metal fell from Ben's hand, the clanging echoing over the stone.

Raven attempted to lift the statue with very little effort. It wasn't as heavy as it appeared. He should go and track Molly, but he'd lost her scent. Once he helped Moody deliver the statue to Laurel, perhaps the boy could help him.

Moody drove a carriage around and Raven loaded the statue in, leaning Ben against the seat. "I'll travel in here so he doesn't fall."

"Very well." Moody snapped the reigns and they traveled along the cobbles at an agonizingly slow pace.

Once they arrived at Ben's office Raven moved the statue into the library as Moody directed.

"What now?" He asked.

"I'll see if I can find some way to pull him out of this state. Can you go to The Horizontal and fetch Mo--Laurel?" Moody asked.

"Yes," What would Laurel think now since her husband was a monster?

* * *

LAUREL HOVERED over Victoria's bed. Tori was unconscious, but her screams had been heard all the way through the streets. Agony wracked her poor petite form.

Sophia started to remove the arrow from Victoria's back.

"You mustn't remove it." Pierre Jean stepped forward to stop her.

Sophia gave him a quizzical look.

"Until a doctor can determine its removal," he replied to her unspoken question.

"My father was a doctor. I assure you I know my medicine. You must all leave. I need space to work." Sophia threw the words out, issuing the command.

Laurel, Count Pierre Jean, and Dominique moved towards the doorway.

"You too, Envoy Kearns, I will call you back once your wife is stable." Sophia ushered Kage out as well.

Once they were in the hallway, Kage laid into Laurel. "This is your fault, and I'll not forgive you."

Laurel didn't blame him. She accepted his anger. "Count, could you please escort Dominique to her room?"

"Certainly, Madam. I will return in but a moment." He eyed Kage warily.

Once the couple was out of earshot, she spoke in a broken whisper. "Kage, I'm sorry. You know I love Tori as much as you do. She is like a sister to me." She touched her hand to his sleeve.

"Victoria is not your wife," he snarled, pulling back from her touch. "All you've ever done is brought sin, slander, and shame to me with this whore house!"

Laurel reeled backward as if he'd struck her.

"Victoria was the only good thing you brought into my life, and now your deeds put her very life at risk. I hope it was worth it."

"You know I never wanted this life," she retorted back. "I was sold, like cattle."

"Did you even once come to me for help?"

She hadn't. As a human, there was little he could do.

"My father is well connected. You wouldn't have had to cater to your queen. I would have protected you." His hands fisted at his sides.

"At what cost? To remain in the harem? To be given away to whichever man your father deemed to give me?"

"These things are irrelevant. You chose to stand alone." He stared at her with cold eyes.

"Kage—" she reached out to him.

The door to the bedroom opened.

Commodore Pembrooke strode down the hall.

"Envoy Kearns." Sophia emerged.

Kage moved his gaze towards Sophia.

"Your wife is dead." Sophia widened the door to reveal Victoria Kearns's pale and lifeless form. The arrow had been removed from her back.

Kage rushed to the bed. He was silent but Laurel noted his shoulders appeared wracked with grief.

The stillness of the room throbbed in her ears. She approached the bed. Laurel felt death at her back. *Too soon. Far too soon.*

Commodore Pembrooke cleared his throat.

Kage stood and turned to Laurel. "You sought no protection and you shall have none." His cold voice lashed at her. "This night, every house of ill-repute will be burned to the ground."

Commodore Pembrooke stuttered, "Emissary, you cannot—"

"This is my city. I can and I will. If you do not assist, Commodore, my men will burn your house as well," Kage replied sharply.

Kage lifted Victoria in his arms. He descended the stairs with a deadly calm.

The front door slammed punctuating the silence.

"Best you gather your ladies and vacate immediately, Lady Gunn," Commodore Pembrooke stated. "Come along Sophia." He grabbed his wife's hand and dragged her from The Horizontal before she could protest.

Laurel stood rooted to the ground until Omar approached, "Miss Gunn?" he asked.

"Omar, you must contact each of my girls and get them out of this house. Have them go to the Embassy and speak with their respective Ambassador. Replace the British flag out front with a white one. The Horizontal is no longer safe."

Omar moved as if on fire towards the kitchens. No doubt Libby was his first concern. Laurel made her way towards the garden to ensure her patrons got out safely. Hopefully, she could prevent any destruction to her house.

She was further deterred by Raven. "Inspector, I do not have time for this. I must vacate the premises immediately."

"I'm sorry Lady, but you must come with me, it's your husband."

She swallowed hard trying to manage a strong answer. "He's The Cleaver." She'd nearly forgotten Raven's pursuit of the killer.

"He is not."

"He's helping Molly?" she tried to keep hopefulness from her voice.

"We haven't found Molly yet, ma'am."

Her heartbeat was listless. It was more than she could bear. All those she loved were gone, taken from her. What was the point of being power-ful, when truly you remained in service to others and powerless?

Her mother, Fatima, and now Victoria were all dead. Molly was miss-ing, taken by a madman. Kage considered her a villain. Moody was little more than a stranger and now Ben. She collapsed to the ground, unable and unwilling to fight. "He's dead."

"It would be best if you came with me." He lifted her from the ground and carried her to the waiting carriage.

CHAPTER TWENTY-TWO

"What happened to him?" Laurel couldn't help but stare at her husband. She ran her hands over the warm green granite stone.

"He transformed into his true self," Moody clarified.

"True self. What is he?" she asked.

"He is a gargoyle."

"Gargoyles are a myth." Laurel had not heard of a surviving gargoyle.

"So speaks my mother, the banshee."

Laurel raised her gaze to Moody. Had he called her mother?

He looked down shuffling from one foot to the other. Clearly, he hadn't intended to reveal his feelings. She was happy the emotions were still there. He lifted his gaze as if wary of her response.

She smiled at him. "We are quite the misfit family, are we not?"

"Yes. We are."

Silent tears fell from her eyes. Would Ben be in this form forever? It seemed damned unfair when her family could be whole.

As tears hit the stone, the surface cracked like an egg. The stone shifted until it was sparkling dust drifting away from the flesh beneath.

Ben reached his hand towards her. "Why do you cry my heart?"

Laurel lifted her eyes in an unfocused gaze.

"I heard your cries. I couldn't bear it. What is wrong?" his cool finger traced her jawline.

"I thought you would be stone forever." Even as she spoke the words, she noticed he still had wings, horns, and an emerald hue to his skin. "Why hasn't he changed back?" she asked Moody.

"I'm not sure." Moody walked to a nearby desk and ruffled through some papers. "I think it might be his heart, preventing the change."

"What change?" Ben asked.

Raven had backed into the far corner, seemingly unable to deal with Ben's new form.

Ben walked over to a glass cabinet catching a portion of his reflection. He turned to Laurel, "Run! You're not safe!" He put his hands up, spreading his fingers wide. The whites of his eyes seemed to swallow their color.

She crossed the room to him, "You would never hurt me." She reached out to touch him.

He threw her hand aside. "You can't be sure. Go! Please, Laurel, go!" He looked away from her. "Look at what I've become. I am a monster, perhaps even the Cleaver."

"Calm down." Moody stepped forward towards Ben.

Laurel watched as her son's hands took on a warm glow. Suddenly a flash of fire and Moody tossed the fire between his hands as if molding it for a purpose.

"No! Moody, keep Laurel safe." Ben backed up until he was against a wall; desperately he clutched the bricks behind him, and dug his claws into the mortar.

"Mother, I need that stone." Moody gestured to her necklace.

"You sent this to me at the sultan's palace." The realization washed over her.

Moody nodded.

"What is it?" She pulled the necklace over her head and gave it to her son.

"His heart." With inhuman speed, Moody reached in and pulled the clockwork heart from Ben's chest.

Laurel watched as Ben swayed before dropping to the floor.

* * *

MOLLY'S HEAD was still encased in the damn burlap. She was tied to a chair, her hands bound behind her. Her feet were tied in front, and the sack was still over her head. She tried to breathe despite her confinement.

Light filtered through the course jute, but not enough to see anything beyond the cloth.

Molly smelled fire and the dust of old stone. It reminded her of the ruins outside of Belfast.

"I'm awake ye bastard!" She shouted.

Footsteps approached and stopped right in front of her.

"So, you are. Are you hungry? I'm about to put a rabbit on the fire." Her captor spoke loudly and the voice felt familiar.

Her stomach growled. Traitorous organ. Hands moved over the knots on her hands and feet. She remained still. The cloth scraped upward on her tender and bruised jawline.

She closed her eyes as the hood passed over them. Once off, she opened them. Dizzying brightness blinded Molly and her stomach flipped as she swallowed her nausea. Molly blinked her eyes a few times, hoping to let the light filter in. It was directly in front of her. She looked to the floor. The light wasn't quite as bright. Molly made out the stone crevices and her own feet; once her vision adjusted she let her gaze assess her assailant.

His boots were black leather, military-style like she'd seen the soldiers wear. He wore black breeches and a long leather waistcoat. His hands were covered by gloves and he wore a shirt, which might have once been white. His face was covered with a dark cloth mask, but his red eyes pierced her. He wore a top hat to complete his sinister ensemble."Hello, my pet."

"Pet? I am not sure if ye know me well enough to infer such intimacies." Molly lifted her chin before pressing her lips shut.

"I'm sorry." He removed his hat, revealing the color of his hair.

NO! It can't be him. Molly's fears were confirmed once the mask was removed, "YOU!"

"Are you surprised it's me, Molly m'girl?" Lieutenant Aaron March had the gall to wink at her before he threw his head back and laughed.

Molly's stomach quivered and her mind froze with the thought that she may not survive the Cleaver after all.

* * *

"WHAT DID YOU DO TO HIM?" Laurel bent towards Ben. The shock of seeing Ben's heart ripped out and replaced with the stone from her necklace was gone.

"I gave him back his heart." Moody smiled after finishing his ethereal stitches.

Laurel was tempted to wipe the grin off his young know-it-all face, but she needed to confirm Ben breathed. She saw his chest rise and fall. "How?"

"His heart was blown out of his chest in Crimea years ago. I kept it until we were captured. I was able to get the heart to Omar through visions and trickery, hoping you could keep it safe."

"I don't understand. My necklace is Ben's heart?"

"Yes. Gargoyles can live without their hearts as long as the organ remains intact. Their hearts are quite lovely in jeweled form."

Her mind was spinning with bewilderment and yet the driving need to have the truth answered propelled her question. "What do you know?"

Moody sighed. "Usually, when gargoyles are cursed, their heart becomes a possession. Whoever holds the creature's heart controls them. The Fae used to bury hearts in castle foundations, so the statues were never able to rise."

"How dreadful, those poor creatures doomed to statue forms forever." Her jaw tightened, the cry in her throat destroyed.

"Yes. In the middle ages, some of the Fae traded in gargoyle slavery. They exchanged hearts and statues amongst each other. Those with wealth, power, and status acquired gargoyles at an alarming rate. It was only a matter of time before the trades were made among humans."

"That's atrocious," Raven's voice shook and his eyes dazed.

"How long will he be unconscious?" Laurel couldn't think how her life may have been different if Ben was one of the unfortunate souls sold into slavery.

"I'm not sure, he's the first gargoyle I've known, and really it was only a suspicion until I saw his transformation," Moody replied.

"As soon as he rises we need to retrieve Molly," Raven commanded.

"Why don't you two go on," Laurel suggested. "I will wait with Ben. Once he rises we will follow."

"Excellent. The inspector should be able to track Molly," Moody agreed.

Raven confronted Moody. "How did you know I could track Molly?"

"You are an inspector, and remember, I met you tracking Ben," Moody said

"I didn't track him. I followed him."

"You must've used your nose when you lost sight of him. It would be very unlikely for a tracker to not use the senses at his disposal."

"You mean a werewolf?" Raven asked.

"So, that's the creature you are," Moody said as if putting together the pieces.

"You didn't know?"

"I have a basic understanding of the supernatural. I've only met a handful of creatures."

Laurel wondered briefly what other beings Moody had encountered. Though she only recently reunited with Ben and Moody, she felt closer to them than before their separation.

"Do you have something belonging to her?" Raven's question broke her thoughts.

"Check her room at the Horizontal," Laurel said. She watched her husband with bated breath.

"Let your nose lead the way," encouraged Moody.

Raven rubbed his temples.

* * *

"You killed five women, including Fatima. Why, Aaron?"

"Who else would cleanse the city of this filth?" he asked.

"The city is what politicians make it. You can't blame those caught in the web of lies and deceit," Molly argued.

He held up his hand as if to stop her. "Is that what happened to you, Molly m'girl?"

"I have other reasons for plying my trade." Given Aaron's delusions, she didn't expect him to understand the sacrifices she made for her family.

"You are perpetuating the problem. If we cleanse the city of its evils, we can start anew." It was obvious Aaron couldn't understand why no one else saw his vision.

"You are delusional." She spat at his feet but missed his polished boot.

"Molly, why don't you give in? I get tired of hurting you." Aaron took a step back, placing his hands on his hips.

"Why me?"

"You are strong. I hoped to align myself with Laurel. She was perfect, forced into the flesh trade by England's queen. But now her husband has returned. She is lost to me now and I must eliminate her." His red eyes bored into her.

"No!" Molly struggled against her bonds.

"Forget Laurel. I have. You are special to me, Molly. You revealed Laurel's true intentions against the Alliance. I couldn't allow that. My mother's family is still powerful, and though England has denied me, I shall seek fortune in my mother's homeland."

"You expect me to marry and go with you to Russia?" Molly was incredulous. His line of thought confirmed he was insane.

"Marriage? Do not be naive. You will go as my mistress."

Her mouth dropped open.

"You should be honored as it is a step above your station of a whore."

"You bastard!" Molly lunged forward, nearly toppling her chair.

Aaron caught her and put her back. He raised his hand to discipline Molly when a voice brought his arm to a halt.

"What are you doing?" A masked woman screamed.

"Does it matter?" Aaron shrugged.

"Yes, you idiot," the woman replied. "I want an army, not corpses. Are you so inept you cannot grasp basic commands?"

Aaron swallowed hard, raised his chin, and fearlessly met his employer's intense look of disappointment.

"Do not look at me like that! You are a soldier, not a strategist. You have no idea what is at stake here. How can I make these people pay for what they've done if you continue to destroy what I need?" The woman approached Molly, gripped her chin, and turned her head as if inspecting her. "I thought your cheek was sliced open?"

"It had been," Aaron blurted.

"How are you healed, what medicine is this?" The woman asked.

"Not medicine, magic," Molly spoke before breaking from the woman's grip.

"Who?" Her eyes squinted hard.

"Moody Jinn," Molly revealed. Moody was a cursed demon. He could protect himself against this intimidating being.

"Interesting, I must find the cause." She turned and walked to the upper levels as if giving them dismissal.

Aaron crouched to meet her eyes. "Molly, m'girl, I can save you from the Master's grip. All you need to do is be mine."

"Master? Don't you mean Mistress?"

"You are wrong. I would never take orders from a woman. Cease your trickery!" Aaron grasped Molly's shoulders.

She thought he might shake her. "Aaron, I'm not sure when you were last with a woman. Clearly, you've forgotten their subtleties. You can tell in the size, stature, and walk. However, in this case, her voice revealed her sex."

* * *

Aaron looked to where his master had left. Could Molly be right?

"Stay here," he commanded. He must get to the bottom of this. Determined to find answers, it took him moments to climb the stairs to the tower.

Aaron didn't bother to knock on the solid oak door. He dared not give Master time to react. He flung the door open.

"What is the meaning of this?" Sophia Pembrooke asked.

"You!?"

"I'm surprised it took you this long Lieutenant. Did you receive help?"

"Molly said—"

"Well, I'm not surprised she figured it out. Men can be such dolts, relying too much on their egos and libidos. Women have much more perspective." She seemed to gloat at his expense. How dare she!

Aaron rushed the desk.

"I don't think so." She raised the whistle to her lips.

Aaron stopped.

"You aren't as dumb as you look." She preened.

"Why?"

"I'm surprised you don't remember. We met after your arm was replaced. My father invented it, you know. It was attached at this very hospital." She spread her arms out.

"Hospital?"

"I know it doesn't look like one. It was a castle. We found it suited his experiments." She drummed her nails on the desk.

"Experiments?"

"Are you only grasping one word at a time? Should I speak slower?" she sneered.

Aaron shook his head. If anything, her identity should have relieved him. How was she more terrifying now?

"My father was a scientist with the Prussian Army during the Crimean War. He worked with diamonds as thermal and electrical conductors. There wasn't much call for his brand of specialty until General Rasputin discovered the technology would work on limbs and organs for the infirmed. He completed the first limb with thermal diamond technology and mercury switches."

"My arm?"

"No, it was a leg, my father's leg. He needed one after the British forces bombed his laboratory. After the war, The Holy Alliance discharged him, but my father wanted to continue his work. So, we moved to this castle outside Constantinople. It was ideal. My father's construction of his own leg was perfect and with the wounded from the war, we were able to continue our work. Since there was no need to return soldiers to an empty battlefield, we conducted experiments on our more unusual patients."

"Why don't I remember any of this?"

"I hypnotized most of the invalids so they would forget."

At his questioning glance, she continued.

"I was a hypnotist's assistant before the war. I was very talented at it, and I've used the skill to get into my subject's mind. You were most interesting and you are only one of two living successes which remain. I'm not surprised you want to kill prostitutes. Your mother was a mistress in the Russian court when your father was there. You must have hated her position to act out and kill these women." Sophia curled her lips and refused to look at him.

"Perhaps I should add you to my list?" It was difficult not to defend his actions.

"You have become harder to control. I suspect you might be suffering from mercury poisoning, and it is affecting how much you respond to my will. Of course, this is handy." She held up the whistle.

Aaron stepped back.

"Implanted under the skin of your ear is a tiny rod serving as a tuning fork. When I blow this," she shook the whistle in her hand. "You are put in an excruciating amount of pain. It is a precautionary feature, nearly all the patients went mad before dying of the mercury." She smiled. "It is rather a shame. You always were my favorite."

"Why can't we be true partners?" He was willing to cast good judgment aside to live.

She laughed, baring her teeth. "I could never partner with a man. Your sex is without trust."

"But you married a man."

Her eyes brightened a bit in their dark depths. "I'm not saying that men don't have their uses. My Emory is merely a means to an end. His rank gives him access to The Embassy's war records. Once I dispose of him, everyone will mourn my loss, and I will live in his house with all of England's secrets at my fingertips."

"But I'm your favorite." Aaron smiled at her. It was the same self-satisfied smile he'd used on dozens of girls plying their trade at Laurel's house.

"I don't know," she ran her fingers over files on her desk. "I'm very fascinated with Doctor Benjamin Gunn these days."

"Whatever for?"

"He is the other living Osiris patient. He survived our clockwork heart procedure. My father was surprised. It seemed unnatural. Of course, Laurel herself is an unnatural witch."

"Laurel is not!"

Laughing, she threw her head back. It was a harsh noise. When she finally returned her gaze to him, "You don't know?" she asked.

"What are you babbling about?" He mumbled.

Her dark eyes bore into his skin. "Hmm, I thought that was the reason you were killing them."

"Who?"

"Fatima, Victoria and the attempt on Molly. You really didn't know? How could you not, they plied their trade, right in front of you? Fatima and her palm readings, Victoria reading tea leaves, and Molly, well she was the most obvious with her collection of tarot cards handed down from her gypsy grandmother."

"Are you suggesting magic? That's impossible!"

"It is very possible and true. You forget I was a maid in that sinful place."

"But Laurel isn't a witch. She's never performed any parlor trick to suggest so."

"Her secrecy makes her more dangerous. The woman predicts death.

In her tea room, she had a large board of Military maps and she could predict the number of deaths on either side of the board. She knew before generals knew. She would write missives to the queen notifying her of gruesome outcomes. I believe Laurel is in league with the devil."

Aaron backed further towards the door until it pressed against his back and splinters of wood pressed into his flesh.

"Aaron I'm not speaking of a war between the Holy Alliance and England," she said, tilting her head down with a frown.

"That is too bad. I'm rather feeling like one myself." He laughed, a hollow sound, even to his own ears. Judging by Sophia raising the whistle to her lips, she must know it as well.

"It is too bad. I liked you, but I need to reform these women to help me deal with the unnatural order which has taken root here."

He watched helplessly.

She pressed the silver tube to her lips.

A piercing cry stopped the whistle.

Aaron released the breath he held.

"Why are you standing there? Go see what it is, you idiot." She shooed him out of the office and Aaron was more than pleased to exit her presence.

CHAPTER TWENTY-THREE

Raven and Moody arrived at the abandoned hospital. The building barely stood. The grand entrance was nothing but columns without a roof and stones threatening to avalanche to the floor below. They followed the columns towards the main arch where the doctors conducted their experiments and the prisoners were held below. Moody should've suspected The Cleaver had ties to Osiris. It all made sense. Why hadn't he put it together? Osiris was the origin of everything evil.

Moody hoped Ben would never have to set place in this prison again, and he'd taken great care to remove any recollection from his father. Moody had stolen the horrific events, plucking them from Ben's mind. Though Ben forgot everything, the moments were not lost. The nightmares remained tucked away in Moody's mind.

Once Raven and he crossed under the main arch, Moody doubled over, grasping his head and crying out in pain. Past memories assaulted him.

"Are you okay?" Raven asked.

"I'll be fine." Moody rested his hands on his knees and inhaled. It was the price he paid for stealing Ben's pain. They became part of him. When the memories held strong emotions such as love, sorrow, or pain - Moody ran the risk those emotions would rule him.

"What's going on?" Raven put his hand on Moody's shoulder.

"The reminiscence of this place is difficult." He didn't feel a need to elaborate with the Inspector.

"You've been here before?" Raven asked.

"I imagine the boy has at least when Laurel's husband was here. Is my thinking correct? Mister Moody, I presume?" Lieutenant Aaron March approached them quickly in long strides. He smiled showing all his teeth.

"How did you manage to track Molly here?" Raven sniffed the air.

"It was almost too easy. Follow me. I'll lead you to her," Aaron said.

Moody found the soldier's manner disturbing.

The way the Lieutenant swaggered as if unconcerned.

Moody's head was pounding, and he couldn't dissect the officer's intentions while at half capacity.

Raven and he resolutely followed Lieutenant March. They passed through the long hall which led them to the large open chamber where the experiments were conducted.

Moody fought the ghosts of Ben's cognitive past. The pain propelled him forward, yet his limbs struggled. Moody saw Ben dragged from his cell and the horrific experiments.

Raven stopped and gripped his arm. "What on earth is wrong with you?"

"It's this place, the strength of the memories. They have a will of their own." It was true. Memories held magic of their own and could affect a human most adverse and bizarre.

"What are you going on about?" Raven stopped mid-stride. Moody nearly collided with him.

"Come along, gentlemen. We mustn't keep the lovely Miss Molly waiting." Aaron turned and vocally prodded them.

Moody walked forward. He watched Raven for signs of unease and hesitation.

The Inspector's steps slowed and his upper lip pulled back in a snarl.

"Is everything okay?"

"The Lieutenant is lying to us," Raven replied.

"How do you know?" Moody's curiosity about other creatures always remained below the surface and he welcomed a familiar field of study.

"How can you not? Lieutenant March hasn't smiled or been cordial to me once in the brief time I've known him. To me, it seems off."

"So merely deductive reasoning. Interesting." Moody made a mental note to thank Inspector Raven for the distraction.

A true distraction lay before them. Miss Molly was tied to a chair and screaming, "Get out! Aaron is the goddamn Cleaver!"

* * *

LAUREL WATCHED her sleeping husband and prayed he would awaken soon. They needed to find Molly before it was too late.

Regardless of his form, she found him beautiful.

His greenish-blue skin returned to its normal hue with spots of freckles. His elegant, soft-as-velvet wings had retracted and folded to tuck beneath the skin under his shoulder blades.

A gargoyle. She had never heard of or seen one alive. She recalled returning to England following her mother's death.

Her father left her to tour the grounds of Canterbury Castle and Westminster Abbey while he handled the paperwork of her ownership. She could not help but mourn those poor creatures trapped like her. It was as if she sensed they were real. She remembered tears filling her eyes before her father admonished her not to cry. Never cry.

Her father wasn't here to stop her now, and she let the tears fall and her heart mourn. Her quiet keening woke her husband from his stoic sleep.

"Why do you cry, my heart?" He reached up and touched the tear falling from her cheek. "This is the second time I've found you like this. Do you cry much now?"

"Only when it is safe to do so," she confessed.

He leaned up, bending one of his knees. "My sweet Laurel, it's not wise, keeping the pain inside you."

She laughed, otherwise she would continue to cry. Laurel's father hadn't allowed her to grieve her mother's death. The tiny girl at the funeral did not utter a single sound. Her father remained stoic, and it wasn't because he'd lost his wife. She remembered people referred to her mother as unnatural, that her father had lowered himself to breed with a banshee. Yet it was the only way to reproduce the coveted fae.

Did her father know Ben wasn't human? No. He couldn't have. Ben didn't even know. Her father had likely planned on arranging a marriage to better suit his aspirations, and Ben had upset his well-laid plans.

She had always felt different until Ben came along. Laurel knew the moment she saw him they were kindred spirits. When he told her stories from the circus, it affirmed his uniqueness. The man who didn't sleep and the girl who didn't cry.

"Did I hurt you? In my monstrous form, did I hurt you?" He grabbed her by the shoulders. He scanned her for possible injuries.

"Ben, I'm fine. You would never harm me, not in your human or gargoyle form," she reassured him.

"Gargoyle? As in stone statues?"

"Moody believes you are a creature of myth, and as you know, he's always been methodical in his research." She stared at her husband's compelling emerald eyes and firm features, looking for a sign of recognition or shock. She saw neither. "You don't seem surprised by the announcement."

"I should be. I suppose years of growing up in the circus and asking how my parents could perform such stunts made me wonder if they were truly human."

"Moody says one of your parents is a dragon, most likely, given your appearance."

"My father, he eats and breathes fire."

"Your mother?"

"She can hold her breath underwater for five minutes or more."

"Moody informed me that fae of two distinct elemental classes give birth to sterile creatures known as gargoyles."

"Sterile?"

"Well that is what he read, but we could try and prove him wrong later." She smiled whimsically.

"Where is our son, anyway?"

"He's gone to help Molly. She was taken by The Cleaver at the rehearsal and Victoria was killed." She muffled a sob in her fist.

"Sophia." His brow wrinkled.

"She tried to help, but she was too late." Her body chilled with vivid recollection.

"Are you certain?"

"Yes. Victoria was badly burned saving Molly. Sophia tried to save her. Why do you ask?"

"Sophia. I know she is somehow responsible for all of our ills."

"Ben, don't be silly." Despite her words, his question brought forth her own doubt.

"I'm not. That dark-haired she-devil is the last thing I remember before blacking out and becoming a monster."

Laurel stood up, "Listen here, Benjamin Gunn, and listen well. You are not a monster. You are the man I love, regardless of what form you take. Do you understand me?"

"Yes, ma'am." He saluted her in a mock ceremony.

"I would like to go find our friends though," she spoke over her shoulder. She strode towards the door. "And you should put some clothes on," she leered at his naked form.

Ben looked at his naked form and laughed.

CHAPTER TWENTY-FOUR

Raven planted his feet on the ground, ready for battle.

Aaron turned to face them.

"Let her go." Moody nodded towards Molly, still struggling and screaming in the chair.

"I don't think so." Aaron raised his right arm.

Raven watched in horror.

Aaron removed his artificial index finger to reveal a blade beneath. It was about three inches long and resembled a scalpel, on his right hand.

"I'll be damned," Raven muttered. The doc was right. Raven had looked for a person with two hands, not one whose hand could become a weapon. How had he missed it?

The smell of mechanical grease from Aaron's automaton limb was prevalent in the air. The stench of it should have been an indicator. Of course, the Lieutenant was already present at Fatima's crime scene, and at The Horizontal leaving Raven's nose contaminated.

"Not yet, but we'll get you there." Aaron ran towards Raven with his weapon arm raised. Raven grabbed the Lieutenant's forearm, and the momentum flipped his attacker over his head.

The villain landed on his back and slid without elegance across the floor.

Raven heard each snag of the man's clothes across the cobblestone floor as the fabric caught and tore.

Moody ran to untie Molly. He turned back to Raven, "Don't you need to change or something?"

"What? No! Don't be ignorant," he turned to answer Moody. Suddenly the hairs on the back of his neck stood on end. He turned back to Aaron, who arose like a behemoth, and his arm piston pumped rapidly, steam billowed from it.

The pronounced vessels in his skin turned blood-stained mahogany. The man's eyes were no longer human. They were blood-red with an eerie lantern glow. The Cleaver stood before them, a killer. There was no longer any part of Aaron there.

"Blessed Mary." Molly stood next to him now moving her right hand in the form of a cross over her chest.

"I thought you were a witch?" Moody asked, tilting his head to the side.

"Now is not the time, Mister Jinn," Molly clicked at him. "What say you, If we survive we share a detailed account of our gifts?"

"Agreed." The young djinn had the nerve to smile before placing his hands together and forming a sphere of fire ready to throw at their assailant.

"This seems rather unfair," a voice behind them called.

They turned to find Sophia Ostwald standing at the stairs with a crossbow in her arms. She fired an arrow off at Molly.

Molly raised her hands. A hidden force deflected the arrow. The arrow hit Moody in the arm and his fire orb went sailing towards Molly catching the fabric of her dress on fire.

Raven rushed to put it out.

The Cleaver advanced.

Sophia retreated.

* * *

"This way," Laurel led the way up the small hill leading to the ruined castle.

Ben followed. They'd traveled quite a distance once Ben released his wings. He had wings for hell's sake. Ben was more terrified of his appearance than his wife was.

When he changed his skin turned a bluish-green hue. The hair on his arms turned a bluish-black hue, matching the guard hairs he'd recovered from Fatima's body. This whole time it had been him. While he didn't fully trust this side of himself, Laurel did.

She merely contemplated him with her secret smile, as if she's always known.

"How do you know where to go?" Ben asked. His voice was deeper, rougher in his gargoyle form.

"Pain and Death," she responded.

"What does that mean?"

She explained in a somber tone. "I've always sensed pain and death. These ruins reek with it."

Ben didn't sense anything foreboding about the building, but there was a tickle in the back of his mind trying to rekindle a lost memory. "Dèjá Vu" as Pierre called it.

"What is that?" Laurel asked, she turned and focused her eyes on him.

He'd spoken aloud. "This place feels familiar."

Without warning, a shadow fell over their path. When they looked up, they found Sophia blocking them. Her ball gown was replaced by a moonstone silk blouse, a crimson corset, black tight-fitting leather pants, matching boots, and a trench coat.

"Sophia, what are you doing here?" Laurel asked.

Ben grabbed Laurel and placed her behind him.

"Dr. Gunn." Sophia aimed her crossbow at his chest. "This explains much. You are a demon of some sort?"

Ben and Laurel didn't reply. There was no reason to give their enemy more information.

"Let me pass." Sophia moved towards them.

"I don't think so." Laurel poked her head around Ben's shoulder. "You are behind all of this aren't you?"

"You should be thanking me. Without me, your husband wouldn't be alive, much less standing before me in demonic form. Although I suppose it is difficult to kill the devil."

That flicker of memory settled at the surface. Iron bars, small cages, and the experiments done on his heart.

He snarled at Sophia and she shot her arrow.

Ben froze, as did his chest. His skin flickered and hardened right before the arrow pinged off his chest, and then with a ripple, the muscles returned to their lithe form.

"What magic is this?" Sophia stepped back, catching her coat and falling backward.

Ben and Laurel advanced on her.

"Stop!" She dropped her crossbow and raised her hands, splaying her fingers wide. "You don't have time to hold me and save your friends."

They halted.

"What do you mean?" Ben asked.

"When I left Molly was on fire. Like poor Victoria." Sophia made a ticking noise, waving an index finger.

"No!" Laurel released an ear-splitting cry.

The sound seemed to vibrate the air around them as well as Ben himself. The tormented yell caused his skin to flicker between flesh and stone.

Sophia grabbed her ears at the piercing scream. Her eyes rolled backward, becoming white. She dropped to her knees and slumped forward onto her smooth ivory face, apparently unconscious.

Laurel's shrieking stopped.

"What was that?" he asked.

"I will reveal myself to you later." She looked down at Sophia's slack form. "Is she alive?"

Ben lowered himself and found her pulse, "She's fine."

"Let us go then!" Laurel pushed past him, marching quickly over the ground.

* * *

MOLLY BACKED UP AND CHANTED. The flames burned through the fabric and licked at her skin. She called forth ghosts, begging for possession. Numerous apparitions awaited entry into her burning form. She waited for a special specter. She was about to surrender hope, but Victoria's soul arrived.

"Raven, get Moody out of here." She nodded to the unconscious Moody who'd taken a sleeping dart meant for her.

"But you're on fire!"

"I'll be fine, I have help coming." Molly went perfectly still. Her fiery form was hijacked by the ghost of Tori.

Even though the flames raced along her skin now and gathered in her hair, she felt nothing thanks to Victoria.

Victoria's enraged spirit took over. The spirit felt no pain and pushed all human emotions to the back. There was no room.

Molly was allowed to bear witness to Aaron's destruction. So she pushed through one thought "There! There is the man who killed you!"

* * *

LAUREL AND BEN walked through the archways to find Raven stricken. He watched a burning Molly grab Aaron about the waist and tumble with him across the cobbles.

Moody lay unconscious.

"Go see to Moody," Laurel directed her husband.

Ben walked past Raven who remained oblivious to their presence.

Aaron shook off Molly, who was now fully consumed or seemed to be. His armor provided enough protection he merely doused the flames which had started.

Molly prepared to launch towards him again, but Aaron used his mechanical arm to hold her at bay by the throat.

Through the flames, Laurel could make out Victoria's spirit as a bright blue heat. What had Molly done? Laurel prepared to advance on Aaron.

Victoria's fire form in his hand screamed, "No, don't come any closer. It's not safe."

Laurel stopped. What was going on? She stepped towards Raven.

"He's The Cleaver!" Raven shouted at her.

Ben looked her in the eyes and mouthed. "He's alive," before he too moved towards Raven's back.

They stood and watched helplessly as Aaron lifted Molly to the ruined wall along the back, that had long crumbled over the cliffs to the water below. There was nothing they could do for Molly. The life force was being squeezed from her. The blueness of Victoria faded before The Cleaver dropped Molly's lifeless form.

Laurel ran to her friend using her own cloak to put out the fire. "Molly, stay with me."

"I cannot."

"No. Moody and Ben can save you. They are magical." Laurel pleaded with her.

"As are you, Laurel. I must tell you-"

"No, save your breath." Though Laurel was glad Molly knew of her origins this was not the time.

"Laurel, I work for the Brotherhood of the Veil." Molly's hands weakly clutched Laurel's sleeve.

"I don't understand."

"The Brotherhood works for Morgan La Fae, queen of the fairies."

"Queen of the Fairies? Molly, you aren't making sense. Be still now."

"Morgan knows about you and she won't rest until she has you. At least with me gone, they'll have to recruit another. I have a request," she rasped.

Laurel nodded.

"Let me go, " Molly's voice faded into hushed stillness.

Aaron turned towards them, "Now the rest of you die."

Raven charged at him but was tossed aside with the mechanical arm.

Ben ran full bore next, letting his wings lift him off the ground and grabbed the mechanical arm, and tossed Aaron into the opposite wall.

Raven stood guard over Molly and Laurel.

Aarons stood, unaffected. He lifted his automaton hand and pulled it off revealing a lance large enough to pierce through muscle and bone. Madness glittered in his red eyes.

Ben retreated towards them. "We need to remove his machine-driven arm. Between his technology and the mercury madness possessing him, he is unstoppable."

Unseen forces pushed Laurel backward and she watched Molly roll off the ledge to the rocky ocean depth.

They scrambled to the edge and searched the darkness.

Laurel saw black. No light and no glimpse of her friends. Her gaze clouded with tears. She wanted an end to all this destruction and death.

Tears slowly found their way down her cheeks. Why must she lose those she loved? Why must she suffer?

Go ahead and cry, a voice whispered to her. The voice sounded very much like Molly.

Let it go, another said, reminding her of Victoria.

Laurel moaned, letting the pain cascade over her. Her long-drawn-out cry vibrated through the room.

Ben's skin rippled under the sound.

She watched, fascinated.

He seemed to flip from flesh to stone and back again.

Raven raised his head and she saw the hair stand up on the back of his neck. His ears twitched.

Aaron clutched his head and screamed. His knees buckled beneath him.

Ben charged Aaron. Once he held Aaron in an unmovable grip, Raven leaped forward to tear the mechanical arm off.

Laurel stopped moaning and her voice lowered to a quieter keen.

Ben and Raven backed away from an unconscious Aaron who no longer appeared a threat. Raven tossed the mechanical arm across the room.

"I wondered what sort of creature you were." Moody was finally roused from unconsciousness.

"What is she?" Ben asked.

"A banshee. She forewarns death and suffering. She clears the way for the reapers."

"You knew," Laurel laughed hoarsely. She'd always felt surrounded by death. It made sense she would lead the charge in front of it.

"It explains why Ben awoke to your crying. Banshee tears have power."

"I was never allowed to cry when I was a child. If I even had a hint of tears, my father would shove a piece of fabric in my mouth and lock me in a trunk."

"Even at your mother's funeral?" Ben asked, his voice soft.

"I didn't attend. I was locked in the trunk the entire day." Laurel knew she should cry, but she was far beyond emotion when it came to her father and her childhood.

Ben moved towards her, enclosing her in his embrace. He folded his wings around them both, creating a safe cocoon.

When he unwrapped her from his hold, Raven approached.

They made their way to leave when Laurel felt metal at the base of her skull.

"I can at least kill you." Aaron hissed. He had raised a pistol in his left hand aimed at Laurel's head.

She stopped cold.

Seconds before the shot was fired, Laurel felt the heat on her back. She jumped forward to escape the fire at her skirts. She turned to find Moody with his hand raised like he'd thrown a ball.

"I'm sorry. Did you not want him dead?" Moody asked.

Laurel closed the distance between them and hugged him with all her love. "I love you Moody Jinn."

She shook her head when she heard Ben and Raven break out in guffaws behind her.

CHAPTER TWENTY-FIVE

*L*aurel approached the building once known as The Great Horizontal.

Kage had kept his word and burned it to the ground.

The second floor was gone. Stone columns remained, charred by fire, along with smoldering pockets where grand rooms once stood. The smell of burning fabrics filled her nostrils and the taste of lamp oil and coal tickled the back of her throat. Her place of business was now burned ash, much like Molly and The Cleaver.

Omar emerged silently from the shadows and approached them.

"Did everyone get out?" Laurel asked.

"Yes, miss."

"We sent all the girls to their respective consulates?"

"Yes, all but Miss Augustine. She is with the Count."

"Thank you, Omar." She dismissed him and turned back to the men who tried in vain to rescue Molly. "I'm not sure where I will go. The loss of this building severs my ties with the queen."

"I'm sure she will understand you had nothing to do with this mess. I can have my superiors speak with her," Raven offered.

"I would appreciate that."

"You don't have to start over." Ben put his hand on her hip, drawing her closer to him. He tempted her with his emerald eyes, but what was he truly offering?

"Since I have no business or home, do you have any suggestions?" she asked, wanting his true intentions.

"Come live with me in my flat." He tugged her away from the group, clearly wanting more privacy.

Laurel stood her ground. He might as well declare himself in front of everyone. "I don't want to stay in this city. If I do, her highness will simply ask me to rebuild. I want out of the spy business and most certainly out of the whorehouse. Also, I don't believe it is safe here. Molly said Morgan La Fae sent The Brotherhood of the Veil after me, and she worked for them..."

"The Brotherhood is a pack of human hounds for the Fae Queen. If Molly worked for them, she was no friend. Did she know you were a banshee?" Moody stepped up to join them.

"I'm not sure," Her voice was like an echo from an empty tomb. She recalled mentioning her gifts to Molly, but nothing specific.

"If Morgan is looking for you, none of us is safe." Moody scanned the shadows, his voice barely a whisper.

"What do you mean?" The idiosyncrasy of her son's knowledge was a bright beacon in the overwhelming and irrational world of fae.

"Long ago Morgan made a pact with King Arthur, and thus the royal families. According to my studies, those possessing royal blood are descended from King Arthur's knights and some of the fae. Possibly Morgan knew about you from Queen Victoria."

"You could come with me to Archangel," Raven suggested.

"That is not a bad idea Inspector. America is not ruled by royalty. In fact, the fae have been fleeing there for hundreds of years. It's probably the very reason Doctor Gunn's parents live there," Moody said in a calm and steady voice.

"Besides, Sophia is still alive and missing, and even if you weren't all creatures of myth, I don't believe it's safe for any of you," Raven added.

Laurel wholly expected to find Sophia on the hill, where she had passed out, but the madwoman had disappeared. "Whatever will we do there?"

"I'm sure they need doctors, and you can do whatever you want." Ben turned her to face him.

"You are an independent and business-savvy woman. Why not enter politics?" Raven said off-handedly.

Ben scowled at Raven before grabbing Laurel's hand and leading her away.

"Are you worried about having a suffragette as a wife?" Laurel asked once they were at a good distance.

"Good God, no," Ben assured her. "You can be as radical as you want, I will absolutely adore you."

"Then why the scowl at Inspector Clarke?"

"Because what we decide is not his business."

"We?"

"Yes, we. If you are willing to accommodate the monster inside me, I'm willing to have the siren in you." He stood before her in human form wearing Raven's coat and his thoroughly ruined pants.

She found his inner beast easy to accept. "Banshee, not siren," she corrected.

"Either way. I love you and I've had enough of being apart."

"Me too." She closed the distance between them and wound her arms around his neck.

"Let us go to Archangel and pave our way in the New World."

"Archangel is under Russian Rule," she said the words cautiously testing the idea.

"If the revolutionaries have their way, it will be an American Territory," he spoke with more than a hint of boastfulness.

"Do you mean for us to join the revolution?"

"I will follow you wherever you go."

We could return to the United Kingdom. I also have relatives in Scotland."

"Does this mean I will finally meet your family?"

"My...you mean my parents?" His arms stiffened and he stepped back.

"Who else? Ben, what is wrong? Are you ashamed of me? What have I done?" She shook free of his embrace and wrapped her arms over her stomach.

He shook his head, vehemently. "I'm not ashamed of you...I..."

Laurel looked at him. "You are ashamed of your... family?"

His face shimmered a shadow of stone tensing his jaw and then back to flesh. "They aren't like you and me?"

"Excuse me dear husband, but I suspect they are exactly like me given the discoveries shared this evening." At times her husband's thick skull belied his scholar's brain. The bubble of laughter erupted from her throat like much-needed rain.

Her reaction seemed to amuse him as the corners of his mouth lifted "I do have relatives in Scotland."

"No. I would rather start new," she conceded. Scotland was too close to England for her. She dare not risk running into the queen or worse her father.

"Shall we then, my heart?" He turned back towards the group and reached for her hand.

"Not just yet." She tugged on his coat.

At his questioning look, Laurel put her hands inside his coat, pulling his warmth towards her. "I love you, Benjamin Gunn."

"I know."

She pulled back. "How?"

"Laurel, when I awoke as a gargoyle and you stared at me without fear, I knew. Your eyes held such concern and love that it was unmistakable." He tightened his embrace and his ruggedly handsome face beamed.

Laurel caught a nearly inaudible cry with trembling fingers over her lips.

"Scream if you must, my heart, but take care of the precious humans nearby," he advised.

She smiled and replied, "Remove your coat and fly me somewhere private."

When he shed his coat and released his wings, scooping her up, Laurel knew her home was with this man. Together they would find their place in Archangel.

THE END

LETTER TO MY READERS

Dear Readers,

I hope you enjoyed *The Courtesan of Constantinople*. If you enjoyed this book, I've included the first Chapter of Book 2 in the Archangel Revolution series, *Alchemists of Archangel,* in the following pages, for your pleasure.

Feel free to follow me on social media. All my links can be found on my website, www.tinaholland.com. You can also sign up for my newsletter there. I only email regarding upcoming releases or deals that my publishers are running.

Thanks again for purchasing this book. Your patronage is appreciated.

~Tina Holland

SUMMARY: ALCHEMISTS OF ARCHANGEL

When scientist Abigail Phelan is accused of murder, she must prove her innocence despite not remembering the crime. Inspector Raven Clark knows Abbie didn't kill the miner, but she is tied to the killer. Abbie and Raven begin a search for both the killer and her memories bringing them closer to the truth and one another. But when Archangel residents fall ill from a bizarre pandemic Raven must hunt for the killer while Abbie battles a ravaging disease. Will they discover the identity of the murderer before losing everything they've found?

CHAPTER ONE

Alchemia, New Archangel (Russian Settlement)
November 1, 1869

"Ouch!" Abigail Phelan cried out at the needle-sharp pain below her navel. She jumped back. The sweeping motion of the heavy silk around her waist held such momentum she nearly toppled off the dressmaker's box.

"Hold still." Emma Flannigan righted her, before placing more pins around the skirt.

"With less than a week away, you'll endure some torture. Why your father scheduled such a late fitting, I'll never know." Emma scolded Abigail. She'd finished the row of torturous pins around Abbie's waist and now began to fold the blue fabric under at the bottom.

Abigail kept her mouth shut. There was no reason to tell the dressmaker she was the cause for the late appointment. At four and twenty, she should handle her schedule but was content to let her father's secretary handle all mundane arrangements. She was conducting breakthrough research in her labs and didn't have time to acquire a new wardrobe, let alone a gown for the ball her father was hosting. She doubted Laurel would even care what people wore to the homecoming ball Professor Phelan was holding in honor of Doctor Benjamin and Laurel Gunn settling in Archangel.

"Will you be in attendance?" Abigail asked.

"With so few females in Archangel, of course," Emma replied.

Abigail narrowed her eyes.

"Don't be concerned, Abbie. Your father is not so rude. He invited all eligible single females including the day-wives."

Day-wives were nothing more than prostitutes. The Holy-Alliance foothold in Archangel had strict laws against prostitution. Ever the enterprising institutions, brothels coined the phrase day-wife. Women were contracted rather than married because there were very small numbers of them. A day-wife was contracted for a day. They were housed by a benefactor, and each house was run by a lawyer who handled all the contracts.

"All the benefactor houses were chosen?" Abbie couldn't imagine her father inviting all the houses, as there were a great many he didn't like.

"He invited Monique's house."

"Monique's Mail Order Brides?" Monique hardly ran a bordello. She ran a house near the train tracks where men could contract life brides. The only catch was women picked their husbands, and after a year the marriage could be annulled if no children were born and the wife didn't find the man agreeable. The period was referred to as a hand contract.

"Yes." Emma chuckled huskily, "you should've seen your eyes widen at the thought of day-wives entering your home."

"I wouldn't have minded." She shrugged and added, "Papa hates lawyers though. He has since lost the patent on his agricultural dirigible to The Alchemist Consortium. It was bad enough protocol dictated he invite the Consortium owners."

"So, who is this Laurel Gunn? Is it true she was a courtesan?" Emma asked.

"Laurel's father was a missionary in India when my father was in the Corps of Royal Engineers. Despite Laurel being seven years older, we played well together, and her mother assisted in my education. I was at a loss when her mother died. Brenna Kavanaugh was the only maternal force in my life and I haven't seen Laurel since the day of the funeral."

"Surely, you've written to each other?"

"No. Papa and Sir Kavanaugh had a falling out following Mrs. Kavanaugh's death." Abigail was lost in thought, remembering the events as a five-year-old child.

"She missed her own mother's funeral, you bastard." Abigail watched as her father raised his hand in a fist as if prepared to strike Daniel Kavanaugh.

"Edmund, you have no idea what kind of abhorrent creature she is." Mr. Kavanaugh shoved Laurel behind him.

"Let me take her then and prove you wrong." Abigail watched as her Papa reached for young Laurel, but his hand was struck aside with such force by Daniel Kavanaugh he nearly toppled backward onto Abbie. She stopped him by pressing with all her weight against his leg.

After finding his balance, Edmund Phelan kneeled beside his daughter. *"I'm sorry, poppet, are you all right?"* He gingerly examined her small limbs and scanned her face for injury.

"I'm okay, Papa." She assured him. *"Is Laurel coming with us to America?"* Abbie looked past the round legs of Mr. Kavanaugh to Laurel whose head was lowered. Silent tears hit the sandstone floor.

"If her father will let her?" Papa raised his face, darkened by wind and sun, to stare hard at Mr. Kavanaugh.

"No, Edmund. No." Mr. Kavanaugh turned to leave, dragging poor Laurel behind him.

"Wait!" Abigail bolted towards Laurel.

Laurel stopped and yanked on her father's hand.

Mr. Kavanaugh released her. He crossed his arms and tapped his foot as if timing this pause in his departure.

"What is it?" Laurel asked, her eyes wet from tears, and a reddening face showing concern.

"I want you to have this." Abigail took a closed fist from her apron pocket and handed over her most prized possession, a tiny pearl ring on a chain that had belonged to her mother.

"This is your mother's," Laurel whispered, looking down at the precious jewelry in her hand. Her lips trembled, and her brown eyes threatened to start more waterworks.

"Don't you cry, child, or I will beat you until you have nothing left," Mr. Kavanaugh whispered.

"You don't have a mother anymore. At least I have a parent who loves me." Abbie knew her barb hit its mark when Daniel Kavanaugh turned on her.

"Did you ever think perhaps her heathen soul was undeserving of love, Abigail?" With the harsh statement, he grabbed hold of Laurel with renewed determination.

Laurel took three steps to each of his long strides to keep up.

"Poppet," her father's voice broke through the cold sinking into Abbie's limbs.

When she turned, he lifted her into his arms and held her close. "That was very kind of you, thinking of Laurel. Never change. You remind me so much of your mother with your generosity." Tears filled his eyes.

Abbie had watched as her only friend was taken away by a man with such cruelty he should never bear the name father.

Emotion brought Abigail back to the present, "I never saw Laurel again. I'm hoping she'll stop by and pick a bird for her hat."

Emma looked up at Abbie with her own watery eyes. "I'm sure she will."

Changing the subject, Abbie spoke up, "I'm very curious about the man who stole Laurel's heart. Papa said he was a doctor. We hadn't heard from Laurel since she married him. Only recently did she reach out to Papa to tell him she and her husband, Doctor Gunn, would be settling in Archangel."

"Where are they going to live? Winter is fast approaching." Emma nodded at the frosted windows.

Abbie shrugged, "If nothing else, we have plenty of room here at the mansion."

"Will you house people the night of the ball?" Emma asked.

"I'm sure we will, we have in the past. Of course, many will want to show off their new steam animals and sleds. Those with money never stay. The miners will, they always do and usually carouse with Papa's cook, secretary, and the maids." Abbie shook her head with a smile, as she remembered the summer festival her father held when the miners reached a large vein of copper. The celebration had extended late into the early morning.

Emma smoothed the skirt down. "There, I think that will do nicely. What do you think?"

Abbie turned around to face the mirror. She liked the color but didn't know enough about fashion to ascertain if it suited her. "If you think it's fine, who am I to complain?"

"The customer I'm making the dress for," Emma answered, staring at her in the mirror.

"I like the color," Abbie said, unsure if she truly did.

"Let's try something else." Emma pinched the bridge of her nose. "Do you have a bird to go with the dress?" Emma asked.

Abbie looked at the silk dress again and the deep blue reminded her of a peacock. Although her peacock Norman was much too big to place on a hat, he shed feathers regularly, and she always kept the feathers to sell to conventional hat makers. "It reminds me of Norman. Perhaps some feathers in a hat?" Abbie pointed to her head.

"I have an idea. Turn around," Emma commanded.

Abbie did as she was told.

Emma went to her reticule and pulled out a pen and paper and began scribbling. Abbie watched fascinated as the process reminded her of when she solved a problem. After a few minutes, Emma approached her, unwinding the tape draped over her neck.

"Stand up straight." Emma handed her the drawing before stretching the tape across Abbie's bottom.

Abbie stared at the drawing of peacock feathers as a bustle on a blue skirt and one long peacock feather in a hat to match.

"I like this!" Abbie turned towards Emma.

"Look straight ahead." Emma pointed.

Once Emma finished measuring for the bustle, she stood in front of Abbie.

"I'm afraid I won't have this bustle done by the time of the ball," Emma sighed.

A few minutes ago, Abbie didn't care and now she couldn't hide her disappointment. "I have a bunch of Norm's feathers," she offered.

"I wasn't concerned about the feathers." Emma waved her off. "I was thinking I need to find the right material to back the feathers and the proper thread for the delicate quills. I'll have to order both. The skirt will be complete though."

Abbie's shoulders dropped along with her chin. What's the point?

"That will be fine Emma," Abbie said. She supposed she could wear the completed dress to the Free Miner's Melee.

"Wonderful!" Emma clapped her hands before gathering up her supplies to see her other clients. Abbie was left alone to change.

"I'll send the skirt to your shop," Abbie said before Emma closed one door.

Emma popped her head back in; "Send it to my caravan. I'll finish it faster. You can send the feathers over too."

The door clicked shut and Abigail stepped off the platform Emma left behind.

She changed with efficiency, not dwelling on the stupid dress. Once in her overalls, she set out to track Norm down for some of his precious feathers.

*

The following afternoon, Abigail was disturbed in her greenhouse by George, a retired miner who served as the household butler.

"'Scuse me, Abbie," he ventured timidly.

"Yes, George?"

"There's a coach, what's arrived at the door." George ran his finger underneath his collar, clearly uncomfortable. She often wondered why her father bothered with the uniforms. The suit was clearly a nuisance to George as indicated by his loosened and sideways bowtie. "Your Pa told us there'd be a Doc and his wife, but there are more folks than what he done told us about."

"Laurel and her husband have arrived," Abbie said joyfully. She removed her gardening gloves and set them down before turning to find Trumbo tooting his trunk at her waist. She patted the brass pachyderm on his head. Unlike most of her father's brass animal creations created for transport, Trumbo's steam-powered head had been replaced with circuits and Teslatricity. He had gone from being a means of transport as a child to something more like a pet as she got older. "Do you want to meet my friend, Trumbo?"

He honked in response. His emerald eyes flashing.

"Lead on George." Abbie gestured towards the tunnel leading to the house.

George led the way through the short cavern, lined with volcanic rock. The Phelan's took advantage of the hot springs and built the conservatory atop one. New Archangel itself had tunnels running beneath the town. The tunnels allowed people to travel in the winter months without venturing out into the cold. Almost all tunnels are connected from the city to the mines.

They entered the house through the kitchen and made their way to the front parlor. Abbie halted and looked at where Laurel and the four others stood.

George turned back to comment towards Abbie. "Told you there was a mess of 'em."

Trumbo held no such reservation as he plodded forward trumpeting his greeting and circling the small group.

"My, my look at you," Laurel leaned down and patted Trumbo on the head, "Trumbo?"

"Yes," Abbie answered, stepping forward. She wanted to run and hug Laurel but held back. The woman in front of her was grown, and though they were once friends, Laurel may not welcome personal overtures.

"He seems different." Laurel cocked her head to the side.

"Papa replaced his steam power with Teslatricity and he follows some basic commands," Abbie responded.

"Fascinating." A dark-skinned young man, not much older than Abbie, said as he came around to peer at Trumbo.

Laurel stood and reached an arm towards Abbie. "Abbie, come and meet my family."

Abbie stepped forward until Laurel captured her hand and squeezed it.

"My heart, don't cry." The man beside Laurel said.

"I assure you, husband, these are tears of joy." She smiled at the auburn-haired man.

"Abigail Phelan, this is my husband, Doctor Benjamin Gunn," Laurel said, releasing her hand.

"A pleasure to meet you, Miss Phelan." Doctor Gunn spoke, wrapping an arm around Laurel.

"The young man covering Trumbo with black ink fingerprints is my son, Moody Djinn."

Abbie thought it odd Laurel had a son not much older than she. Abbie figured she would hear more in detail later so she didn't press. Trumbo enjoyed the attention, flapping his ears, and tilting his head from side to side.

Moody stood, wiping his hands on his pants, before extending one to Abigail. "Sorry about that." He nodded to the fingerprints on Trumbo's head.

"It's alright.   I'll have you help me polish his head, and then you can learn how he works if you like."

Trumbo apparently liked the idea, as he knocked Moody's hand with his trunk, an indicator to pay him some attention.

While Trumbo monopolized Moody's time, Laurel introduced Libby, her maid, and Omar, her manservant. Unlike George, Abbie was not intimidated by the group's size. She planned with the staff to see them settled.

Almost an hour later, she knocked on the room where she had placed Laurel and her husband.

"Come in," Laurel called.

Abbie opened the door to find Libby unpacking a valise and running items to the bureau and dresser. Omar stood guard by the door and towered over Abbie as she entered. Laurel and Ben turned from looking out the window.

"Enjoying the view?" Abbie asked.

"Yes. Doctor Gunn and I were just discussing building."

"Oh?"

"Who owns the land adjacent to you?" Laurel asked.

"The Alchemist Consortium and the Free Miners own most of the land. Papa bought his land from the Free Miners. As part of the arrangement, he agrees to provide every miner with tools of their trade. We have tunnels off the south side of our land."

"Are there any abandoned mines?" Doctor Gunn asked.

"I'm sure there are, but none surrounding our lands. Perhaps Papa can be of assistance. He's familiar with all the mines. You can ask him at dinner. I'm afraid I'm going to be getting my birds ready for the ball and all the ladies' hats." Abbie confessed as she rattled on.

"I must stop and view your lovely animals, perhaps bring Moody along," Laurel said.

"Moody seems fascinated with Trumbo. He's spent the afternoon in the kitchen commanding Trumbo to do various tasks. I think Trumbo enjoys the attention."

"But he's a machine." Doctor Gunn said.

"True, but he seems quite capable of learning, and the engineer, Sam Brownsmith who mounted the circuit board, was very talented. Sam programmed all the brass mules to haul rock and ore out for the free miners. The mules follow basic commands, perform weight calculations, and do purity tests on the ore samples. They are an upgrade from the Jumbos and other brass animals you'll see the night of the ball."

"There are more brass animals?" Doctor Gunn asked.

"Yes, but they are like the Jumbos my father built in India."

"The ones in Constantinople are much the same," Laurel stated before a smile spread over her face.

"What is it, my heart?" her husband asked.

"Wait until Raven sees all these animals. He is going to go absolutely mad." Laurel smiled at her husband.

Doctor Gunn threw his head back and laughed heartily. "Oh, he hated those elephants when we were packing them up to head to the docks. This will be such a treat." Doctor Gunn chuckled and kissed the top of his wife's head.

"Who is Raven?" Abbie asked.

"Inspector Raven Clarke. He invited us to come here with him," Laurel said.

"Will he be staying here, too?" Abbie asked, wondering if she had time to settle in another room.

"I believe he was looking for lodgings in town. He was hired as a sort of constable." Laurel said.

"Sheriff." Doctor Gunn corrected.

"I heard the free miners were looking to hire a private detective. They believe the constable is in the pocket of the Alchemists," Abbie said.

"I will mention Raven to your father and if he hasn't already made arrangements, we'll see to it," Laurel assured her.

"Very good. I'll see you at breakfast then?" Abbie asked.

"Certainly," Laurel and her husband answered in unison.

Abbie couldn't help but smile as she shut the door. As she'd watched Laurel and her husband, their closeness caused tightness in Abbie's chest. She was sure she'd never had a relationship with the opposite sex where they stood on equal footing. Sam Brownsmith taught her men didn't respect women who worked in their realm. Men seemed to question everything, whether they were smart enough, talented enough, or could swing a hammer. Granted, mining was hard work and most of the miners were men, but to resign the women of Archangel to a few small careers – if one could call time spent on their back a career – was stupidity personified.

Putting on her coat Abbie shrugged off her anger. She headed out to her coach steam-powered by a pair of brass horses who creaked and stomped as if ready to get underway. She grabbed her cage of avian samples and donned her father's old Busby and made her way to the coach.

Once inside, she punched in the coordinates on the panel in the front of the coach and the horses took off at a trot. It was the optimum setting.

You could set the coach to gallop, but it required more coal in the beasts. She didn't have time to use the walk setting, as she may already be late.

She looked forward to sharing the new samples. The doctor she was meeting with did some wonderful work with men who had been injured in the Alchemist run mines and laboratories.

Abigail gathered up some of the iridescent colored canaries which changed color to camouflage into the background. They were nearly invisible. The doctor was looking for a less intrusive way to monitor her patients. Abigail had trained the canaries to sense problems and change color to indicate an emergency. She and Trumbo worked with the Canaries on how to detect distress in patients by interruptions in breathing, increased heartbeats, and even skin discoloration. On display was an ideal home for her canaries that were not quite suited to the mines.

Her carriage came to a slow smooth stop and she stepped out, walking to the boarded sidewalk, and knocked on the door at the end of the long street.

The door opened, and she was greeted. "Abigail, I'm glad you could make it, come on in."

Abbie took in the white apron with some spots of blood and said, "I can come back later Doctor Pembrooke."

"Nonsense. I've finished with my patient. I insist you come in." Doctor Sophia Pembrooke stood aside, granting Abigail entrance into her small office.